SAM THE CAT

MATTHEW KLAM

PENGUIN BOOKS

PENGUIN BOOKS

Published by the Penguin Group
Penguin Books Ltd, 27 Wrights Lane, London W8 5TZ, England
Penguin Putnam Inc., 375 Hudson Street, New York, New York 10014, USA
Penguin Books Australia Ltd, Ringwood, Victoria, Australia
Penguin Books Canada Ltd, 10 Alcorn Avenue, Toronto, Ontario, Canada M4V 3B2
Penguin Books India (P) Ltd, 11 Community Centre, Panchsheel Park,
New Delhi – 110 017, India
Penguin Books (NZ) Ltd, Cnr Rosedale and Airborne Roads,
Albany, Auckland, New Zealand
Penguin Books (South Africa) (Pty) Ltd, 5 Watkins Street, Denver Ext 4,
Johannesburg 2094, South Africa

Penguin Books Ltd, Registered Offices: Harmondsworth, Middlesex, England

First published by Viking 2000
Published in Penguin Books 2001

2

The stories in this work were originally published in the *New Yorker*. 'Issues I Dealt With in
Therapy' and 'European Wedding' were published in different form.

This is a work of fiction. The characters and events in it are inventions of the author and do
not depict any real persons or events.

Printed in England by Clays Ltd, St Ives plc

THIS BOOK IS FOR
LARA COX

Contents

Sam the Cat . 3

Not This . 29

The Royal Palms . 65

Linda's Daddy's Loaded 95

There Should Be a Name for It 123

Issues I Dealt With in Therapy 145

European Wedding 193

SAM THE CAT

Sam the Cat

WHAT YOU REMEMBER about an old girlfriend is perfect. Even the horrible parts are fine. Especially when you don't have anything else going, the memories of her are lethal. In my office I have an ad from a magazine hanging above the desk. It's of an old girlfriend who is a model, and I've been thinking about her for days. It has been a long time since our paths have crossed, and for that I humbly thank God. But I think if I had her here right now I'd marry her.

All of my girlfriends wore their hair the same way—long and straight, with bangs in the front. They all liked sex, they were all good-looking, they liked the same kind of music I listen to—Rolling Stones, Little Feat, the Who. They all kept up with me, drinkingwise. They all had their own cars.

What was wrong with any of them? Paula was small and dark and depressed and smoked a lot of cigarettes. Sarah

was a ski instructor, too full of herself; she pissed in the bed when she drank. Irene had a knowledge of the New Age and did aura paintings and collected herb-tea boxes. Holly's eyes crossed when she got tired. She was chunky and slept twelve hours a night. Boots had an interest in anal sex but acted lazy and as unimportant as a secretary. I went out with a Japanese girl, Makiko, who threatened to break up with me if I didn't carry a clothes dryer up four flights of stairs to her apartment. And I dated a fashion model named Ann—the one in the picture—who was actually bald because of a rare disease. Was I asking too much? I wanted real love. Where was that loyalty and trust? Where were the laughs? Under a rock? Inside a chocolate-chip cookie?

I wanted real love. Not a replay, not the same thing over and over again, not the same dinners, that same let's rent a video tonight. I wanted love and everything—cut flowers, her wearing a beautiful dress, lingerie, seeing an incredible band, blow jobs in a convertible. Going to Africa for Christmas—you know, the finest champagne, meeting movie stars together, amazing parties with a see-through dance floor. How many times do I have to hear myself explain this?

In the picture above my desk Annie is modeling a leather motorcycle coat without her wig, totally bald. The weird thing is that we went out for almost a year and I never saw her without the wig until I opened the magazine.

One time she asked if I wanted to see her with it off, and I said no. See, because her wig was what first attracted me to her. She looked so incredibly hot, dancing in a tank top with this gorgeous long black hair, and what a nasty little surprise when I find out it's somebody else's hair.

I get this feeling looking at the picture of Annie—a warm, sour sensation under my sternum. I know what that feeling is: that I did something wrong, and the reminder of guilt is deep and uncomfortable, but it's more than that. Because when I look at her eyes, staring off the page and looking at me but not seeing, I almost want her back. It's not a joke. I'd do anything to get her back. If she called me on the phone right now, I'd drop to my knees and I'd cry.

"Sam," she'd say, "would you be my boy?"

She's just starting to smile in the picture—that amazing wide mouth of hers sliding open, her eyes pointed down like she has a secret. I need her to want me again. Then, once she says I can come over, and later looks up from down there with those big brown eyes that drink you in, I'll want to get out. And I won't want to see her or talk to her or listen to her voice on the phone.

What is that, Sam I am? I ask you: Is it love? Because if it is love, the world needs a little bit less of it.

You know what? I fucked her. She's done, she's dead now, so fly away. I did Ann and her sister and their fat friend. Ann went to Germany on an important assignment. She wrote me postcards from the Hofbräuhaus. I called

her friend up on the telephone, we ate moo-shu pork and drank and had sex with my pants pulled down on the lawn beside my car.

Hairless and tan, rich and slutty—for all her unique traits, Ann does not hold a candle to Louise, my most recent girlfriend, the only person in my life I've ever truly loved. Louise seemed to really know me and, despite that, wanted to be with me. But she is party to the situation I am currently avoiding, and so I make do with the perfection of memories. I know what's going on—it's all a big cycle. I've had a girlfriend since I was in second grade, and I'll probably have one until I croak. The problem is, despite my current confusion, which I'm coming to, I love, love women. I like to see them bark for me. That's a joke. I love having a girlfriend. All they ask for is a normal degree of fidelity, and then they'll let you do whatever you want to them. Anything. You can have them bent sweetly over the back of the sofa with their gorgeous ass in the air and they won't say a thing, because the truth is everybody digs it and just needs the excuse of love. I get myself into all kinds of trouble, all that rubbing in the dark. Rubbing and rubbing in all those beds next door to a church or over a health-food store or in the back of her mother's house. I bet if you put them end to end, I've rubbed my hand across bare stomachs from here to Estonia and back. They give the word and it's a free-for-all. If I were a girl I'd fuck ten guys a day. I swear. I'd never want to be a girl, though, for they have the worst deal in history.

You are looking at the original hopeless lover. I love it all, the first few phone calls, her hair in a bandanna, getting drunk together the first time, seeing her teensy underwear. The normal pit in your stomach is replaced by a whirling feeling. Then those beginning-couple weeks together, where you're sort of thinking about it no matter what else you're thinking of. There's no ruminating about what to live for when the alarm goes off before work in the morning. You find a long hair of hers stuck to the sleeve of your suit, and you hold it up to the light. For the next ten minutes you are stoned, picturing last night. You take her to a really fancy restaurant for dinner, you go shopping together, you go on double dates, you decide whose house to sleep at. You call her on the phone and then call back—"One more thing . . ." One evening after another is righteous. It's nice. You're her boyfriend now, nobody else calls. She starts to talk rotten about her old boyfriend. You meet her friends, you meet her family, you say what your kids will look like, you think about marrying her.

I love being in love. I'm so in love, I'm so in love. Sometimes I don't even know what I'm in love with. I'm in love with the love drug.

You walk into a supermarket or a restaurant, your girlfriend goes in first and you're looking at her ass. And you say to yourself, "Isn't that the most beautiful ass? That's mine. It's beautiful." Like it's going to save you. An ass isn't going to save you. What's it going to do? Hide you from the police? Call up your boss when you don't feel well?

• • •

MY GIRLFRIEND LOUISE and I went to a party—mostly advertising people I knew through work. It began late and followed a long day where all I wanted was a simple meal in front of the TV. But I knew I'd hate myself if I missed it. Things happen at parties that your friends talk about for weeks, sometimes for years. You can't miss them. You can't get in on a great joke after the fact.

The party was held in a refurbished warehouse. There was a band in one corner, guys carrying trays of hot hors d'oeuvres, and a cash bar. They had a hateful mime walking through the crowd. I was mad at myself for going, disappointed at the turnout, and pissed that I'd brought Louise, because she didn't know anyone. When people asked about work I explained that the Mafia had hired me to do P.R. I acted like a prick to let them know there were better places to be, but at the same time I was forcing out jokes and clever observations because I wanted everyone to like me. That's why I go to parties. Anyway, people like you better if they think you don't like them.

Louise and I started bumming cigarettes off people. If they said yes we'd ask for four. And then she waved hello to this girl who was heading up to the bar. I couldn't see her well because of how dark it was, but she stood over six feet, with silky, jet-black hair just above her shoulders and hanging around her face. She had on blue jeans and a T-shirt, a high, tight athlete's ass, small knobby shoulders so that she was almost cocky-looking, but very skinny with

those sharp hipbones that you can feel right under the bikini. It was too dark to see everything.

I wanted to have a chat with her. "Louisie," I said, "when you go to the bathroom I need you to check my phone messages."

"O.K.," she said, and I handed her some money. She left, I went hustling up to the bar, wangled over to this chick, whipped on my best head fake and grin, and it was a man.

He had some high cheekbones, he wasn't broad, maybe he could be one of those handsome, pretty male models you see in Calvin Klein ads. I don't know—I'm not an expert on how guys look. Yes, right, a basically handsome guy. Up close, though, I saw that he needed a shave. He probably had had sexual relations with Louise sometime in the past—that's why she waved.

He was a skinny dude with long hair, that's all. Not a woman.

When Louise came back I told her—not that I went running over there but that when I saw him out of the corner of my eye I thought he was a chick. We screamed. I'm such a turkey sometimes I don't know why the hell girls go out with me. That's the real mystery.

I am a fantastic lover. I've got to give me that. There are only two things about me that females don't like: the fact that I sing when I drive—admittedly, I'm not a musician—and my skiing. All the girls I know ski moguls well—really solid bump skiers—and I try to turn in the swells and lose

my downhill line. I have thick hair, I've got a car that stinks from new leather. My skin, my body—that's all decent. But I get ridiculed on bumps, and the way I sing gets mistaken for a joke or an imitation of someone dippy, when in fact your car is one of the few places besides the bathroom where you can sing the best songs the way they were meant to be sung. They all think my singing is terrible. Screw them. (I did.) You sing in the car because it feels good, you can't help it, and because you know the fucking words. Everyone I've gone out with—it's like a secret tradition they pass down from one to the next behind my back— laughs, then puts her hands over her ears, and after a while gets huffy or angry when I sing. I confess I'm not a professional, but I'm at least trying. You know, I wish I had some say in what traditions they pass from one girlfriend to the next.

What is it with me, though? I mean, I lie, I fuck whoever will let me, I can never remember the name of her best friend, and I hate to dance. I will, I do often, I volunteer, but it makes me sick, and I end up sweating too much. I come off with my shirt soaking, probably because I'm so out of shape. I attract a crowd of people who can't believe how bad I am. Like the worse I act, the more they want to be around me.

By the time Louise and I left the party, the liquor had done things. I kept running into the curb on the way out of the parking garage. I went home and shut my eyes and tried to sleep, except there was this guy, the guy who

looked like a chick, walking around the party in my mind. I watched him walk up to the bartender, I saw him reach into his front pocket to get money, and I saw how his round butt stuck out a little—somebody stop me—and I was horny, so horny I couldn't believe it. I kept thinking about it and squeezing my legs together. Just his butt in his jeans. I'm like tingling. I actually wanted to whack off to him. See, in my mind he was sort of a woman, but—What do I want to say here?

I made myself fuck Louise. I didn't want to—and she was the very picture of unconscious—but I had to. I'm a man. Any man would do the same. The next morning over coffee and cereal, I asked her how she knew this guy, what was his name, where did he work. Now what? Was I all of a sudden gay? I went to sleep one night and woke up a homo?

Put yourself in my place. I had to clear my head. I had to forget. The next weekend I went away on business, and the one after that Louise and I and two other couples borrowed a friend's cabin for a quick getaway. We drank the liquor, made a pizza with psycho mushrooms, Vicky and Tom's dog got run over and killed, the waterbed Louise and I slept on somehow got punctured, and the night of the bathing-suit contest Tom left the Jacuzzi on and burned out the motor. The cabin was a short drive from the city, though. Sixty-five or seventy miles north on the interstate.

A few days later we were having drinks at Sid's Rat, short for Rathskeller, and the guy—his name was John

Drake—came in. He was a housepainter. He ran his own company, and he also played in a band a lot. Louise knew him because her old roommate had some connection to the band.

"There's your friend," she said, and we both laughed. Louise waved hello and offered him a seat. I shook John's hand. We talked about the usual bullshit. Louise mentioned his band, and he said something about it going O.K. He seemed like a pretty cool guy, very normal-acting, with pale, light-blue eyes. Maybe he was half South American or something—his skin was a light-caramel color. His face was what you'd call angular, and when he smiled his face changed, since his teeth were perfect and very white. His hair was thick and straight and shiny black. I realized then that I'd seen John around before: he plays hoop at the rec center where I play hockey. Our leagues meet Tuesdays and Thursdays in the rink downstairs. I've seen him outside the gym.

John had to leave. We met some people from an ad agency I'd never heard of. They taught us a game called Upchuck, which uses dice and shots of Cuervo. Just as I started to get the hang of it, my leg became tangled in a bar stool and I fell down and chipped my tooth.

Later we were lying in Louise's bed, getting reacquainted, and I was trying to picture what John's house looked like on the inside. I wondered whether anything in my house needed painting. Louise gently implored me to lie on top of her, and I saw his butt again in my mind. He

had on different pants that night—tan khakis—and a faded blue denim shirt. You could tell he was very slim and in shape. There I am, horned out and at the same time queasy with the weirdness of it. Sam the cat, he bad and naughty. He dirty kitty-cat. I felt like I was hairless and twelve years old again, caught wanking in my mom's closet. I thought the cops were going to come in and bust me, because they should've.

A BIG ACCOUNT threatened to leave our agency. Our creative team had to fire up a new campaign—radio, print, and television. We got it done at the wire, the campaign went over well, and I personally got the thumbs-up from my boss. The client rep took everybody out to a Japanese place. We dined on platters of sushi and bottles of Scotch. I was in a very chipper mood and even went in with another guy on an eight ball of Peruvian blow. I wired myself right up, high and tight and feeling no pain.

The last place we visited was this fake cowboy bar. It was late and the place was kind of empty. Two couples were dancing. The band up on the stage was still playing. I guess they had to stay. I bought an overpriced, watery pitcher of Bud and wandered around with it in one hand and a complimentary bucket of popcorn in the other. The cocaine had actually been cut with talc, I could tell from the taste, and it wore off fast. But something in that sushi acted like tequila worm on me, and I found myself in the mood to dance. I checked out the field but there wasn't any, so I

kind of slanked around by myself. They were playing some twangy country song. The guy's voice was the kind you hear on the better side of country and western, if there is such a thing—deep and clear, without that disgusting yodeling break in his high notes.

I went ahead and started dancing, beginning with a redneck-style hop-skip, like you might see on *Hee Haw*. Then the hop gave way to the spin—I perfected a certain type of spin—splashing beer and popcorn in a circle around me, effecting sincere consternation in the other *danseurs*, and I looked up onstage and it was him.

John was the lead singer. This was the band Louise had told me about. He also played the violin, or fiddle, or whatever the fuck it's called. I stood there on the dance floor. He seemed pretty intent on the music and didn't look at the people too much. I started to get into it, sensing the country rhythm, doing a sliding move here and there, with a shake to it. I did a spin, bumped into somebody, and lost the popcorn, but I kept my eye on him and went up close to the stage to dance. I danced up and back and snapped my fingers. I yelled "Hey!" up to him. He nodded and gave a half wave, and then, when the singing part of the song ended and it was just the instruments playing, I shouted up that it sounded pretty good. He motioned to me that he couldn't hear. I moved as close as I could and yelled up that when he said he played in a band I didn't think it was a country band. He made a face and looked away; maybe he didn't understand. I yelled up that they probably did

Elvis tunes, that it sounded like Charlie Daniels, and he turned to the guy playing the guitar and sort of laughed. I screamed up at him that I knew a lot of people who might get them gigs, but he was looking above me, straight ahead. I told them that the guitars sounded excellent, that all kinds of people liked country music, that when they were done if they wanted to get a beer I might be willing.

I WOKE UP in my bed, with my coat and tie and shoes still on. It was Saturday morning. I took everything off. There was dried barf on my shoes. I'd puked in a urinal at that cowboy bar—that came back to me. And when I went over to try to talk to John while the band packed up their equipment I fell over a stack of drum boxes. On the way back home a wheelbarrow somehow got stuck underneath my car.

I went into the kitchen. The downstairs smelled like cat piss. Skippy's litter box was like an overflowing minefield. I poured a bowl of cereal and a dead beetle fell out, though when I touched him he started to walk.

I lay on the living-room floor and read the newspaper. There were leaves and sand and pubic hairs in the rug. Skippy's fur was stuck around the coffee-table legs.

I looked in the mirror. I had blackheads on the end of my nose.

I vacuumed, bought food, did the dishes, purchased a bilevel shag-carpet kitty facility for Skip. It cost seventy dollars. At first he refused to acknowledge it, but as the day

went on I saw him jumping up to the carpeted box on top, pretending it was a cave, and chewing on the fresh, new-smelling carpet. I napped, cleaned my pores, called my girlfriend, and rolled a bone. I played an old jazz record my dad had given me and watched a movie on Cinemax. For the first time in a year I went to bed before midnight.

Sunday morning I looked in the phone book and found out where John lived. I put on a decent shirt and pants, shaved, and started over on foot, since it was only about half a mile away. I had on a new pair of loafers that were shiny and uncreased and cut into my heels when I stepped. I went into a 7-Eleven and got the Sunday paper and a thing of flowers. In front of his house I paused to check myself in a car window. I looked fat and pale but well rested, and honest. I walked up the steps to the back door. It was not yet 10 A.M., and knowing he might be asleep I sat down to write a quick note of apology.

I heard somebody going around the kitchen, the refrigerator door slamming, and water running. When I looked in the window I saw a man standing behind the table looking at me. It was John, trying to figure out who I was. He opened the door and said something I couldn't make out and stood there watching me. I said, "I turned over a new leaf after Friday night and I'm apologizing to everybody I offended lately."

He held the door open, leaning halfway out. His light-brown skin showed against a white V-neck T-shirt. The door spring creaked. It sounded like a bird with a long

neck—maybe a goose—being strangled. I stepped back, attempting to get a better stance, and placed my new loafer in the dog's water dish. It was a sign from God of something rotten.

Nobody deserves anything. But if there's such a thing as retribution, at that moment I was living it, paying myself back in the form of humiliation. No one, no one I've ever known, would've believed that act, me standing at John's door with the bouquet of flowers, hoping he'll take them. Drum roll, then Sam the cat he takes two dainty steps and nose-dives off something very high.

He told me to come in. I reminded him about yelling up at the band while they were playing. That didn't ring a bell. I mentioned falling over the equipment. I said, "At least I didn't puke on you." Then his memory of me came back and I handed him the flowers. He kind of laughingly went and showed them to somebody in bed in the other room. A woman came out with him and we were introduced. Her name was Barb. I'd never seen her before. John asked if I wanted coffee, and while he was making it Barb went behind him to toast some bread and placed her hand on the small of his back. He told me all the drunk stories of playing music in bars as she went from the toaster to the refrigerator, John's eyes following. Barb poured some coffee for herself, he handed her a spoon, and she went back to bed.

The stories he told made what I did seem minuscule, or at least average. I told him you get sick of acting like that after a while. There's no dignity in being a slob.

The conversation turned around, and I told him what I do, writing radio and TV ads for an advertising agency. I said the next time we needed a country band for something I'd call him, and he gave me a card for his painting company with the phone number on it. It had the address of this house, and in quotes it said, "Ask for John."

I went home and cleaned more, ironed dress shirts for the week, and trimmed my nose hair. I turned on the TV and thought of John, images of him walking around his kitchen covering over the show on the screen. I switched it off, because in my mind John was doing this funny dance—similar to what he did with his hips onstage playing the fiddle—in his smart, well-fitting jeans. I got up out of my chair and started to do my own dance in response. I clapped my hands and spun around, put on a Stones album, and hopped across the rug. I found the silver bracelet my mom had given me for my birthday and slipped it on, combed my hair back with gel, and stared at myself in the mirror, holding my stomach in and flexing my flabby, skinny arms.

IN ADVERTISING YOU have hectic times with everybody running at a frenzy for weeks. It ends and you get horribly slow times, and management begins firing the less talented people. Account execs go out for lunch and don't come back, secretaries fill the garbage cans with old files. I make pictures of Garfield using the X's on my typewriter, my office mate calls telephone sex lines. I couldn't stand it after a day and got John's card out of my wallet.

The card in my wallet was like a revolting story people had found out about me, like I took nudie pictures of children. You want to run around erasing the story from everybody's minds, but events happen in your life that cannot be erased. The fact is, these events change you forever. You're not the same person anymore. You're someone new with the same name. You don't feel better, as in "New is better." You're somebody new but you feel mucky. Hopeful, but with a sour feeling down below.

I left a message on John's machine that I wanted to talk to him about a commercial we had in mind with a country-western theme. I said we needed a band and I'd call him that night, and hung up fast.

At home I cooked dinner for myself. Louise asked to come over, but I made an excuse about work. There wasn't anything left to clean or vacuum, so I played with Skippy. He kept scratching me accidentally. We weren't communicating very well. I was getting more nervous by the minute about making that call. I finally did, though.

John answered.

"Hey, John, it's me," I said.

"Me? Jim?"

"This is Samuel Beardson," I said. "I left a message on your machine today. I was the guy who came over Sunday."

"Oh, yeah, sure," he said. "What's the word?"

"Well, as I mentioned, our creative director, Chuck, wants to use western music on this Juan's Tacos frozen-dinner commercial."

"Tacos?"

"Selling tacos," I said.

"Should I write a song about tacos?"

"No, don't do that," I said.

"Just kidding," he said.

"Oh, sure," I said, and laughed.

"I don't know any songs about tacos offhand."

"Ha-ha," I said.

"Why don't I mail your office a demo tape and you or the other guy can tell me what you think," he said.

"Good idea. That was your girlfriend I met, right?"

"Oh, yeah, she's someplace—"

"Girls—I mean women—it's a crazy thing!" I said.

He said, "I think she's down in the basement doing her laundry."

"Really? How long have you two guys been living together?"

"About two years," he said. "We're married."

"Girlfriends—you need more of it or less of it, it's hard to tell which. Know what I mean?" I said.

"Yeah," he said. "It's tough."

"That's right," I said.

"It's tricky," he said.

I told John, "I could write a book on everything I know about girls. There's so much we don't understand. She cries for no reason, the guy gets angry, one of you is always on the defensive."

"Yeah," he said, laughing.

"It's like some weird kind of a religion," I said.

"I'd take a woman over religion any day," he said.

"Me, too," I said. "You ought to come over tonight and I'll give you my full explanation."

"What?" he said.

"I should write that book," I said, "and give my full explanation."

"Yeah," he said. "That's a fine idea." Then he laughed.

We said a couple more things and hung up.

AFTER WORK THE next day I drove to the mall. I walked into every store. It was like wishing you were hungry so you could satisfy the craving, but what food would you want? Not chocolate, not booze, not salty or sweet, not cheesy, not ice cream, not chips.

A men's boutique had some loose, blousey shirts on sale, with rounded cuffs and pleats on the shoulders. I bought a tan one. I bought some navy pants made of a thin material, and a pair of flat black shoes. Then I went down to the department store and got some new hair gel and some cream that's supposed to tone your skin.

The woman behind the counter was in her fifties. She had a pretty, narrow face and a pointed chin, circular, drawn-on eyebrows, maroon lipstick, and a stiff yellow crown of hair surrounding her head like a plastic lion's mane. I asked her what a model would use to maybe improve his look. "If you want to look the way average men look, then go home. You're in the range of expectation."

She took out a jar of white cream and a tray of what looked like pastel crayons. "But if you want to look better, sit down in that seat. Let's give you some zest. Let's give you some pep. Some sex appeal."

"Sounds good," I said.

She held a red crayon up to the light. "Let's give you a touch of masculine pizzazz."

"O.K.," I said.

"That's the way you wear your hair?"

"What do you mean?"

"Too flat," she said, fluffing up the front part.

She showed me an eyebrow darkener, to make the brow stronger, she said—more expressive. I leaned over the counter, and she gently drew a tiny black brush through my left eyebrow. I watched in the mirror. Then she did the other one. With each stroke I looked more and more like my sixth-grade football coach, Mr. Gaspari. I held her wrist. "That's wonderful," I said, "I don't want it on me now. Just tell me what to buy."

They had a cream to make it look as though you were tan, and a lip moisturizer that makes the lips a deeper red. I bought those and something you brush on your eyelashes, because mine barely exist. She gave me a special sponge to start with and a powder-finish thing that goes on last. I bought another powder, too, for drying up excess moisture. I paid with my credit card, and she said, "For touch-ups!" handing me the bag.

I suppose I thought if he saw me, if he and I took a walk

and caught a glimpse of ourselves passing by a store window, I would know something then. I would know what to say. This wasn't a guy-girl thing. That is to say, this wasn't a sex thing, no. Not entirely. It was also a third thing I keep trying to describe. Maybe spiritual.

I took a shower, shaved, and did everything the way the woman explained. I used the sponge first, did the eyebrow stuff and then the tanning cream. Put it on the neck and ears? I didn't know. I brushed some of that junk on my eyelashes. It clotted up and fell in my eye. I had to take out a contact lens and flush my eye over and over until I finally got the gunk out. I applied the powder finish last. I put on my new clothes and shoes. The pants were my normal size, but my big ass barely fit, and then I ripped the seam trying to straighten them. They were brand-new pants. I grabbed my wallet. There were no pockets in these pants. They were smooth in the front and back. What do you do with your wallet when you wear them—shove it up your ass? I went out to the car. The seam ripped more as I got into the driver's seat.

Behind me headlights came up the driveway, blinding me. It was Louise. Now her car was in the way. She got out and headed for the front door, but she spotted me in my car and walked over. I rolled down my window and said, "Hey."

Louise bent down and looked at me at eye level. It took a few seconds. She said, "Hey, Sam," scratching her upper lip, the place where the soft white hair is thicker, an area I

told her she should get waxed. She was smiling, but her smile was getting weirder and weirder. "Ha," she said.

"Ha-ha," I laughed back. Nobody could think of a thing to say. She could have said any number of things. "Have you looked in the mirror lately?" was what she said.

I lifted an eyebrow to play along. "That's what I was just doing," I said. "Is it on right?"

"Sam," she said, but it was more like a question, the beginning of a question.

"I made a bet. I have twenty minutes to get back to Sid's Rat and sing to these guys to collect."

"What guys?"

"The bartender."

"You look like Sinbad," she said.

She looked at me, at one eye and then the other eye. Back to the right eye, back to the left. "I bet you're lying." Her voice was muddy in her throat. She looked one last time, her hands on her knees, ducking down to the open window. "God," she said, "you lie so bad," not knowing if the way I looked was a joke or not, or where it might be leading.

"Don't be ridiculous," I said. "I haven't done anything wrong."

"We haven't seen each other in two weeks," she said.

"Louise, take a pill," I said.

Louise coughed and pulled a tissue out of her pocket. "What am I doing?" she said, and she stood up. I was left

sitting in the driver's seat, staring at her fly. Her hips turned toward the house and then toward her car. Then she was gone.

I went back inside and took the clothes off. I put them in a paper grocery bag and got back in the car in jeans and a sweatshirt and headed over to the rec center. That hoop league John played in met on Tuesdays and Thursdays, the same as my hockey league, and I wanted to be there when he came out.

A fountain stands by the entrance, and cars drive up to drop people off and pick them up. There are streetlights that make everything bright, and I stood off to the far side of the building, where it was darker, out of people's way. I paced back and forth, checking each time the door opened to see if it was John coming out. I still had on that lip stuff and everything. I looked strange, I bet. A tan, pretty Coach Gaspari. I must have seen two hundred kids with hockey equipment, chopping their sticks against the sidewalk while they waited for their moms to come get them. Finally the basketball players came out. At the same time a few guys from my hockey team came out the other set of doors, all sweaty, carrying bags of equipment. I'd forgotten about this possibility. They came down the sidewalk toward the parking lot behind me. I tried to figure out how I could intercept John without my teammates seeing me, but there was no way, so I took off at a run, not stopping or listening to hear if they saw me, and got out my keys and bolted.

· · ·

DURING THE FINAL phone call it kept going silent, with me not saying anything. John didn't know what I was thinking. How could he know? I thought I might be getting a peptic ulcer. My father got a peptic ulcer at age thirty-two. I said, "Your band is great."

"Thanks," he said. "So your office got the demo."

"Yeah, the way you sang on it was terrific," I said. "You could sell anything with that voice."

"Appreciate it," he said.

I can't remember what else I told him. But then I said, "Can I ask you a question?"

"Shoot," he said. "What?"

"Hey, would you come over tonight and I could make you dinner?" I figured if I just said it. Because it was that or not say another word.

He said, "This isn't about the tacos, is it?"

"I could make tacos."

"Are you gay?"

"What?" I said. "No."

"Forget it," he said, and hung up.

"Forget what?" I said, but I was too slow.

I didn't want to do anything with him. I didn't even think of sex with him. It didn't enter my mind. Well, of course it did. But to hang around John, the two of us sitting there together—that would mean something to me. He'd call with some funny thing he had to tell me. Then I'd know. Then we'd both know. Maybe he'd ask if he could

borrow something and I'd say yes. Or the two of us could get a video. It's not a big deal. I don't have to explain this. It's obvious how I felt.

I FEEL NEW, but I don't feel shiny and clean. I feel older, newer but older. It doesn't make sense. The new me feels old and heavy. Watching TV makes it worse.

I have the memories, crisp ones, of every moment of love that's ever touched this flesh. The elegant photo of Ann in my office is among these reminders. I sit at my desk at work and every few minutes go back to it. The way her mouth begins to open, with her eyes cast down shyly so that if you stare you begin to wonder what she's thinking. I must say it's a skillful ad. What else would I need? Lately it seems I can't get close to anyone without offending her. Or him. I keep trying to call Louise. She takes the phone and puts it near the Cuisinart I gave her last year—set on pulse/mash, it sounds like—so I have to hang up. Of course Louise still turns me on, but what do I do? Go over there half gay and start kissing her? Joseph, her roommate, would take one look at me and know something's not right. And what about Joseph? Not my type. What am I saying! Mother of God, listen to the way I'm talking.

A week has passed since John hung up on me. My house is so neat. I washed the kitchen floor last night on my hands and knees. I should take photos of it. If I had a family I'd get everybody down here now, dressed up, and take the Christmas-card picture before the place got messy again. If

I were married and had kids. But where would I get a Christmas tree this time of year? And who would I marry? I'll tell you who I should marry: myself. With my cat Skippy as the mascot. We could sail around the world together. I'd get Skippy a tiny yellow rain suit. "Man the mizzenmast, you little furry wog," I'd say. "Get me a halyard." The ship would be my kingdom. I'd have a sword and an eye patch, some movies on video belowdecks, for when the wind dies. I'd love the seagoing life. Maybe out there I'd come across something I could understand.

Not This

Am I a good person or a bad person? I'm not a great person—I know that. I've been a certain way my whole life: Mr. Showcase, Mr. Jokey, Mr. Handshake. After a while, even I can't stand it. I look down on people. I've got a short fuse. I piss on my friends. I always thought the benefit of being this type of guy was that you forget the things you do to people, and you go on living in a happy pink bubble. You're not such a winner, but you're allowed to forget.

I had gone over to Kiffany's with the idea of persuading her. I took the gun. I have a confession to make: As a kid I was fascinated by Nazis. I hated them, like everybody else; I would think up tortures to pay them back—gouge out their eyes with a rusty fork, rip off their balls with pliers and shove them down their throats—but I also thought they were terrible and dangerous and, so, worth thinking

about. I drew swastikas on my notebook. I ordered a catalogue of war paraphernalia from the back of a comic book, and in it were wool uniforms and spiked German helmets, Third Reich binoculars, leather holsters, and guns—cigarette lighters made to look like guns—and, after all these years, I still had the gun I got then. It was a lighter that looked like a .45, the American gun. It was fun to use. A big flame came out of the barrel. At my place, Kiffany lit her smokes with it seven times a night. It was big and heavy. It looked real.

I had on a T-shirt and gym shorts, the elastic waistband of the shorts bulging and stretched out. I had one hot, red ear from an hour on the phone with Kiffany, who lived two blocks away, more toward downtown New Haven, and I'm running over there in my flip-flops with this gun tucked into my shorts. Don't ask me to explain the state I had reached by the time I headed over there. Sometimes love is not what it's cracked up to be. I had this idea of using the gun as a prop, actually to lighten the mood of our quarrel, like, "Why don't I just kill us both? Why don't you just shoot me, or I'll shoot you?"

An old guy in a station wagon had his turn signal on and was pulling toward me—I realized then that I was walking across his driveway—and I hurried up a step so he could turn. The gun fell down my shorts. It hit the ground and broke. They said it was identical to the real thing except for the lighter mechanism. Obviously not. The old man looked

at it and looked at me. I grabbed the three biggest pieces
and ran up to Kiffany's house and went in.

We started in on the same fight we'd been having on the
phone. Kiffany said, Hold me; Kiffany said, Let me go. I let
go of her, all right. I was frustrated, and we were both so
tired of fighting—I let her go kind of through a doorway,
like, Get away from me, so she could maybe go sit in the
other room, where it was cooler. Except the door was
closed—a swinging-type door with no knob. I forgot to
look, and she found that out with her nose. Well, more her
forehead. Afterward, we both cried and she put ice on it
and I left and went home and she didn't press charges on
me. That's when I knew it was time to take a break.

My brother called then. It had been a while. Dave's my
older brother, and I could tell him my problems. He lis-
tened. Then he said he had a reason for calling. He had
something to tell me—good news. I said I didn't think
there was any good news left. He said, "Hey, Vince, Denise
is pregnant."

"Wow—shit," I said.

"What do you think?"

"That's a major event," I said.

"We're pretty happy," he said. I asked him how long be-
fore it would pop. He said seven months.

"You got enough money for it?"

"Yeah."

Dave had been really busy. Getting married and a new

house on the Jersey shore and a new job. We weren't as close as we had been. Everybody was so wrapped up with work that we hardly ever called each other. We waited too long and then had nothing to say.

I hadn't been to their house since Christmas, and that was the first time I'd seen it. Dave had met Denise two years earlier, taking golf lessons. Then, in the span of eight months, they got engaged, set a date, joined a church and a health club, got married, bought a house, and now she was pregnant. We hung up, and when I thought about that call I could picture Dave touching her belly.

They live near the water. Some things are automatically picture-perfect. It dawned on me that the weather down there is always mild, and with Labor Day coming it might be a nice idea to visit them. "Uncle Vince"—it clanged like an old, familiar bell. I called him back. I reminded him of the troubles I'd been having with Kiffany, and said that since there was a holiday weekend, I was thinking of getting out of the city.

"You're saying you want to come down?"

"Maybe. I don't know—sure."

"Let me ask Denise," he said. "I'll call you back."

"Thanks," I said. "Fantastic."

"I'll call you back."

"Hey, how far are you guys from the water?" I couldn't quite remember.

"Not far," he said.

"Is there gonna be a picnic or anything?"

"A picnic?"

"Like a Labor Day picnic."

"I don't know of any picnic."

"I'll bet there's something in your area—a street fair or a sack race. I haven't been to a picnic in ten years."

"Let me call you later."

It would be an opportunity to get away from this scene for a while. To be there at the start of their adorable family—my timing was exquisite. Later, Dave called and said it was O.K. So I put some stuff in the trunk Friday morning. After lunch I got out on the road and turned south.

KIFFANY WAS THE last in a long line of failures. Looking back over the years, I could see a pattern. Pictures came into my head on the road to my brother's house. Old faces drifted across the road in front of me, things I had done. I looked for a good station on the radio. The drive was about four and a half hours long.

Kiffany was the best-looking, the smartest, the best dressed. She had gone to Harvard. A lot of people go to Harvard. I didn't. They hired Kiff in marketing at the radio station where I worked, the second-biggest station in the city. She got the job through a connection. I'd been there for four years, and I was the chief engineer. It takes about ten seconds to tell whether you like a person, and when I saw her that first day, in that dress, I thought I could learn to love a woman like that. She was tall and skinny, she wore

cool clothes, her chestnut-brown hair was cut short and fresh. Look at that face. Her cheeks were smooth, and the tiniest white hairs stood out against her tan skin. She had big, pink gums that were evident when she smiled. And tits that were full and moved as though they were either very firm or sheathed in leather. Go ahead, I thought. Why not? We could become friends. She had just moved here from somewhere else, and I'd show her the town.

I found, upon reflection, that she fit my idea of the supreme woman. Why? Who gives a shit. I felt love.

We went on a few dates. I got to see another side of Kiffany, away from the station. She cared about people. She helped at a retarded-kids' sporting event; there were photos and T-shirts to prove it. Soon, we never spent a minute apart. We were a couple now—a thing.

Then we hit a rough spot. Someone was always on the defensive. After a while, we couldn't watch TV without that dead silence between us, making everything tense. The weeks went by, and the weeks turned into months and then into a year; soon it was Halloween, with New Year's right around the corner, honking at us like a paper party horn, and we stuck it out a little longer. We stayed apart for a while, the misery died down, and we got back together again. It was easy—and at the same time it sucked shit. One night I locked her cat out of her apartment. It meowed at me through the window, and I gave it the finger and left it out there.

I told Kiff, the day I bruised her forehead, "I love you.

I'll do anything for you." I wanted to take her somewhere private and apologize and fill her with my cement.

"As long as you get your rocks off, right?"

See, I couldn't affect her. She was too intelligent. I came off as the dumb one, and when I finally got her attention, it was charity. I don't know when I began to realize it, but she made me feel ashamed—for the way I ordered food in a restaurant or for what I wanted to order. Or for talking too much to the waiter—that embarrassed her. I'd joke about something and the waiter and I would laugh, and instead of laughing, she'd stare at me, blinking. Other times, around her, I'd sit there smiling fakely, acting like the perfect boyfriend, and then I'd realize what I was doing, and I'd get furious. I'd think, What the hell am I—her slave?, and haul off and take a cheap shot at her. "Sorry," I'd say, eating a piece of apple pie she'd baked. "This crust tastes like glue."

Before Kiffany, I went out with Diana, who was pretty and liked graveyards. Before her was Lisa. We never got out of bed—she never got out of bed. She never did anything except watch TV. I dated Jessica, who had rosy cheeks and flat, oily hair, and who called me my darling, my Vincent: "Could you hand me those potato chips, my darling?" Shut up. These girlfriends, they seemed to like me—sometimes it could be described as love—for anywhere from nine months to two years. I dated a girl named Kurt, who was gorgeous and rode a mountain bike. She was a lesbian but made an exception for me—she explained

the switch in a long letter written on tracing paper in purple crayon—it didn't last, though. I had girlfriends as far back as nursery school. Look at all the years, and all the women, between then and now.

AS I PULLED into Dave's driveway in Cape May on Friday afternoon, he and Denise walked out the front door and stood with their arms around each other, watching me park the car. I went over and gave my brother a hug. He said, "Hey." He messed up my hair. I kissed Denise.

"We're pregnant," she said, and kissed Dave's face. "Vincent, I'm so glad you're here."

"I know," I said. I went to the trunk of my car and they followed, arm in arm. Dave grabbed my suitcase, leading me toward the front door. I looked around. Their house and the yard were looking tidy as hell—rigidly manicured lawn, blooming flower beds. On my way up the driveway I'd passed a new mailbox with their names engraved on it.

"The place looks unbelievable," I said.

"Business is cranking," he said.

"It must be," I said.

"It's nuts," he said. "Come on."

He showed me his office setup. I saw that he had a new computer. There was also a laptop, two cell phones charging, new carpeting, and a big leather couch.

"Jesus," I said. Dave waved me on through. The living room looked different. "Check this out," he said, leading

me toward the kitchen, and as we went through it I could already sense a big change—there was all this light, it looked totally screwy—and then we turned the corner, and there was a big, glass-walled addition they'd put onto the back of the house. There were plants and a leather reading chair and a glass dining-room table. The floor was made of tiles. "Wow," I said.

"Great, huh?"

"Yeah," I said. "You didn't say anything—why didn't you tell anyone anything?"

"I wasn't sure it would happen," he said. "It was kind of down to the wire. It got sort of tricky. The builder is a client."

I nodded. We looked out the window to the yard. I said, "Is that a trampoline?"

"It's a minitramp," he said. "Denise works out on it."

"Aha," I said.

"She's got to have that thing to work out on every day."

"Sure."

"I don't want her using it now, because of the baby," he said, and he smiled. "Anyway, it'll have to go someplace else. We're putting in a pool there."

"A pool? In the ground?"

He had his hands behind his back, staring straight ahead at the yard. With his baseball hat and his sunglasses, he looked like an army colonel.

"Right out there," he said. He kept looking straight out.

"Fuck, man, what are you selling—drugs?"

"Image," he said. "I make a boring business into something you can love."

Denise showed me to the guest room. It was still the guest room then, but soon it would be the nursery. I could already picture the little Finster in his room here, spitting his cookies on the floor.

She said they had had some tests done that day at the doctor's. They were waiting to hear. "We want to make sure everything is in the right place. We don't want any surprises." I said, Of course. She leaned against the doorjamb, her long black hair pulled back. She had on a sweater and blue jeans. I asked her how everything else was. She said it was what she'd always hoped for, they were happy.

I put my stuff away and showered. I checked the cable channels. Denise shouted for me to go get the grill started out back. Dave was still on the phone in his office, with the door closed. The grill sat between two garbage cans, behind a box for recycling. I wheeled it a safe distance from the house, went back in, found some matches and lighter fluid, and got to work. Behind me, the sun was starting to set on their neighborhood: Labor Day weekend, barbecue, the whole American scene. I waved to their neighbor, who was wrestling open a patio umbrella. The guy waved back. I was glad I'd come.

The charcoal lit on the first try. The flames went six feet into the air. From inside, Denise yelled, and when I looked up, sooty chemical smoke was pouring through the screen

door into the house. I went over and shut the sliding glass door. I wasn't going to leave the fire unattended. Dave came out and, without speaking, got a garbage-can lid and dropped it on top of the fire.

I said, "What are you doing? What the hell?"

He pointed his thumb to a large object standing beside the glass doors, covered by black plastic. He was panting. He said, "We have a propane grill. We don't use that one anymore."

"Oh," I said. He walked over and lifted up the plastic cover. I said, "I didn't see it."

He said, "Were you planning to burn down the neighborhood?"

"It's supposed to be a big fire."

"The propane one is safer."

"O.K."

"All you've got to do is click the thing here. Let me do it. Why don't you go unpack, man?" It was a new deluxe stainless-steel grill. I watched him press the button, and I went back inside.

Dinner that night was amazing: some of the best salmon, everything carefully put on the plates, baby asparagus and shredded yellow something; stuffed clams, eggplant on the new propane barbecue with a marinade, fancy California wine. Denise had become this vicious cook. She'd baked rolls, and made this cheesecake with a design in it. She said she'd taken a class at the high school and then gone back and taken all the other classes.

· A friend of Denise's joined us—a woman Denise had met at the health club, who owned her own vitamin store and wasn't married. Her name was Jen. She had frosted hair—it stood up on her head like a bird's wing—and throughout the evening she regaled us with health-food stories. I could see they liked her. She was short and harmless. She talked about the color of healthy urine, and they both joined in, and for a while the discussion at dinner was about urine. Any ailment, anything that ever went wrong with anybody—Jen had had it once, too, and had the answer for it in a vitamin.

In the kitchen Dave said, "Jen's got an incredible body. Sometimes she comes over and works out with Denise. You should see the fucking outfits she wears."

"Wow."

"She gives lessons on the banjo."

"No shit."

"You should go for it. Ask her out for tomorrow night."

"That's O.K.," I said. "Pass."

After we ate the cake, I said good night. It had been a long drive. Dave folded the newspaper and gave it to me. He explained to Denise and Jen that when I was a kid I used to always read for a while before turning off the lights.

SATURDAY MORNING, I woke up at ten and lay there, in the strange bed in the guest room. I'd slept twelve hours. I stared at the walls, glad to be out of my apartment, waiting until I was ready to get up. I'd dreamed a hundred differ-

ent wacky dreams that night: my parents were sucked up in a hurricane, Kiffany was my sister and had a tattoo on her butt, a tidal wave came and washed Dave's house away. At eleven, I heard Denise and Dave come in the front door. I went out to say hello. Denise passed me. She'd been crying so long that her face was swollen. She said good morning and disappeared into the bedroom.

Dave went toward the kitchen. I followed him. He filled a glass with water and drank it in one gulp. "Ahh," he said, and burped a dog bark. I was sitting there in the T-shirt and shorts I'd slept in.

Except for the sunglasses and the baseball hat, he looked like our grandfather. He put the glass on the counter, laced his fingers together and laid them over his stomach, shrugged one shoulder and then the other, like our father, and bit the inside of his mouth. He stayed like that, chewing on it.

"What was that?" I said.

He looked past me, toward the part of the house Denise had gone to, and filled up the glass with water again and drank it.

"You want me to get out of here?"

"No," he said.

"What's the deal?"

"There's no deal. Denise is disappointed—that's all. The doctor had the results for the tests. We just got back from there. She's not pregnant, for one."

"Oh."

"We did a home pregnancy test. Then the doctor did another test to confirm it. It came out negative." He filled the glass again.

"Geez."

"She has some chronic infection—there could be complications."

"Huh," I said. "Oh, boy." I got up and looked for a glass. Dave handed me one. I opened the refrigerator. "What kind of complications?"

"They said the infection comes from some kind of bacteria. If it's serious, she can never have kids. It would make her infertile."

"God. How did she get it?"

"She had an IUD when she was in college, and it might be from that."

"I bet you feel terrible."

"It's all part of the deal. It's not worth talking about."

I took out the orange juice. Behind the opened orange juice they had two unopened backups of juice set to go. Unopened backup jars of everything. In the bathroom that morning, I'd seen fifteen bars of Ivory soap under the sink and a case of toilet paper standing beside the john.

Dave said, "You hungry? I'll get Denise to make you something."

"No, I'm fine."

"Did you eat? Were you waiting around for us to come back before you made some food?"

"No, I just got up."

"What did you eat today?"

"I said I'm not hungry."

"My house is your house—anything here. You know that, don't you?"

"Yeah, I know."

"Toast yourself a bagel. Or—look, there's muffins here." He pulled some bags out of a drawer. "And this onion-bread thing. We've got seven boxes of cereal. Look at all this bullshit. Do you like milk on your cereal?"

"No, I like piss. Of course I like milk."

"Eat something. Now."

"O.K. Stop it. Stop talking about food. Shouldn't I do something to help?"

"Forget it. We have doctors for that. You're our guest, Vince, and you're my brother. You make yourself something to eat. Or ask Denise. She loves making food." He poured another glass of water.

"All right," I said. "Sure."

"Good," Dave said. "I love you, Vince." He walked out of the kitchen with his sunglasses still on and the glass of water in his hand.

LATER THAT DAY, a truck pulled up and guys unloaded six chaise longues for the new pool that wasn't there yet. They were going to start work on the pool very soon. My brother walked out with the phone on his ear and pointed the men to the back of the house. I put my magazine down and tried to talk to them in Spanish. We pulled the plastic

wrap off the pillows. The new chaises were made, I believe, of wrought iron, which had an intentionally aged look to it. These chairs weren't from any K mart. They were beautiful. The armrests had dainty patterns engraved in the metal. Each one weighed about a thousand pounds. There were big white cushions that went on top.

Dave had them set the chairs up in a row—along one side of the pool, I guess—all facing toward Denise's mini-trampoline. The only other thing back there was a bird feeder. Now, though, six people could recline in the sun and watch Denise bounce up and down. She's lovely, my sister-in-law. My brother would kill me, but I've got to say it: He's always had amazing taste. Denise was a full-time aerobics instructor the first time I met her. That was a couple of years ago, but she's still very athletic. She has a narrow face and high cheekbones. Her skin is dark and tan, her hair is long and thick, shiny black. And she's got tits like in a dirty video, and a beautiful, round, heart-shaped ass— oh, man! Anyway.

I went out and sat in one of the chairs. I brought a magazine with me, but for that entire weekend I was so exhausted that every time I sat down I felt it—as if someone had sewn lead weights into my clothes. I was tired from stress. So I opened the magazine and passed out in the sun.

When I woke up the sun was farther down in the sky. Dave was beside me, with his laptop and his phone, reading through some papers. He had on his baseball hat and

sunglasses. Denise was a few chairs down, in a crocheted bathing suit. I yawned and stretched. The afternoon sunlight came streaming through the trees. Pollen dust drifted in the light, and it made sunbeams. It looked magnificent— a person could contemplate the entire universe from here. I said, "God, this is so neat."

He said, "We like it pretty quiet."

I said, "Look at the light."

"I looked," he said. "Particles." He was reading, holding his chin.

I said, "Wow—it's like a postcard."

"Yeah, postcard," he said. "You snore."

"I only snore when I'm really tired."

"You always snored. How can anybody stand that? It sounds like you're drinking a milk shake through your nose."

I asked him what he was reading, but he started telling me about his public-relations business. Dave worked for himself. He said he'd acquired a specialization, and that he was putting together "a multimedia attack" for the client.

"Wow," I said. "Sounds big. How's it going?"

"It's going good."

"Well, hooray. What else are you working on?"

"I don't have time for anything but this right now."

"Uh-huh," I said. He nodded. I said, "I'm sure that'll change." I gave him the thumbs-up.

He shook his head. "This is my only client."

"Oh."

"No, Vin—you're not getting it. I dumped my other clients. I just work for these guys now."

"I see. Is that the way to do it?"

"Yeah, it's the way to do it. How the hell should I know?" He was pissed. He said, "I already told you on the phone."

He explained that the client's company was basically four businesses: waste management, construction, a muffler-and-shock-absorber chain, and an investment company that oversaw everything. He'd done freelance stuff for them through a bigger agency, and then at a meeting one day they asked if he would do PR for their company full-time. "I do everything for them—buy all the media, deal with the ad agency. A family owns it. An Italian guy and his brother-in-law run everything. Real sullen assholes."

"Really," I said. "What—no cement company?"

"Ha. Don't say that too loud. They probably have this place bugged." He laughed.

"I know. Christ, you're working for the Mafia."

He wiped his eyes with the palm of his hand and said, "But look—they're gonna make us a pool," pointing with the telephone.

I looked at the area set aside for the pool. It's hard to tell how something will be when it's finished just by looking at the ground. It would catch a lot of shade from the house. "Wait a second," I said. "Where's your sewer line? Did you get a permit for this?"

"We don't need a permit."

"Sure you do. You have to have a building permit."

"Not with these guys."

"But wait a minute—that's crazy."

"No, it's not."

"What's going on? You have to have a permit. You have to declare all this."

"Look at Mr. Painfree here, giving me advice."

"I'm not giving you advice," I said. "Stop and think about it for a second, though. You want to put yourself in that kind of position? You're leaving yourself vulnerable."

Dave yanked his glasses off, accidentally bending them at the nosepiece. He said, "Look who's talking, fucknob. You're going to offer me advice? Your whole life is fucked up. Your last girlfriend was a bed wetter."

"Only when she got drunk."

"Well, whatever. It's great getting advice from you, man."

The phone rang. Dave answered it. Denise got up then, and walked into the house in her bikini. Jesus. She was ridiculous. "Yeah," he said. "I'll hold." He put his hand over the receiver.

I said, "My whole life is fucked up?"

"I don't want your advice," he said, and unbent the sunglasses and put them back on.

LATER, I DECIDED to go for a run behind their house. Dave told me where to find trails along a defunct canal. The woods matched his description, but the trail would

open up and then take a sharp turn and end. I'd hike over some bushes and find it again, or maybe it was a different trail.

Everything was wet—the ground, the leaves. Dank and slushy. No wonder they'd built a canal back there. It seemed like the whole area was below sea level. It smelled like rank mud. It was spooky. It reminded me of how, as a kid, I was always scared. At school I was scared of other kids beating me up. At home I was scared of my dad. At night I was scared of falling off my bunk bed onto the record player. I was a coward. I took a sharp turn and slipped and fell. My hip hit a tree root, and it hurt. I got mud on my leg—the mud was black. I remembered how much running sucks. I lost the trail completely and didn't have the common sense to believe I'd find it again a few yards up. I limped around, dirty, looking for the trail. My heart was racing.

THAT NIGHT DAVE and I dined alone.

It was more of the same, excellent food—fruit salad, homemade bread, bouillabaisse—but I had no cheerful set-up date this time, and Denise skipped it completely and went to bed. We sat there in silence. Dave was in a sour mood. I was thinking about other things. His problems were not my problems, and he had a whole lot of problems. That call earlier had been from his employers. When he hung up, he looked as if he was about to cry. Well,

guess what. Tough shit, asshole—it's your life. You picked it. Nobody forced him to work for a bunch of gorillas.

Dinner was kind of grubby, the two of us reading the newspaper at the table, not talking, cutting farts. I picked my teeth and flicked the stuff on the floor. It was depressing. Goddamned morbid. Then, after dinner, Dave did more work. I read my magazine. It just depressed me more. I wanted to help somehow.

I got on the phone and made some calls, looking for a Labor Day celebration. After an hour, the closest thing I'd found was a Norwegian party at the Rotary Club on Sunday and a keg toss Monday at a horse stable. Then Dave came and sat next to me in the living room—he said he couldn't think. I showed him the address of the Rotary Club. He said you had to be Norwegian to get in.

Finally, we talked about their fertility problem. "It's in the doctor's best interest to scare us, but Denise probably just has some minuscule infection that they can clear up in a week," he said.

"Of course."

"Denise is a physical specimen. She comes from a healthy family."

I agreed. I thought he was right.

But what if they were unlucky and there was damage, Dave said, and she couldn't have a child? I asked if he'd leave her. "No," he said, "and if she ever left me I think I'd die." Then he went on to name the options. Adopt a

baby—he figured they'd qualify as pretty fit parents. Or find a host mother and give her some money. Or—he didn't know—no kids and more hobbies.

"Sure," I said.

"I'll buy a moped."

"I don't think they make mopeds anymore."

"I mean, this is the whole reason we got married and rushed and bought the house—for the kids." I nodded. He bit his finger. "Maybe it's my fault. We've been trying for a while." I didn't say anything. "A long time."

"How long?"

"I'm getting worried."

"Don't worry. There's nothing wrong with you."

"How can I be sure? Nobody ever got pregnant from me." I was nodding, trying to be understanding. "Maybe I'm shooting blanks. Maybe I took too many drugs in college."

"What drugs?"

"I smoked pot."

"Pot doesn't do anything."

"Think about all those gay guys out there with good sperm who don't even use it."

"They use it."

"How do you know?"

"What's that supposed to mean?"

"It wouldn't surprise me. It's the only thing with two legs left for you to conquer. Anyway, Denise and I were

talking—if there's something wrong with me and we need a donor, would you do it?"

"Do what?"

"Be the donor, shithead. In the event that mine's defective."

That thought hadn't occurred to me. We do have two sisters, but that's useless in this situation. Dave didn't say anything. He had a sad look in his eyes.

"Whatever you need," I said.

"We'd have to test you for everything. No offense."

"Yeah," I said.

"Good," he said.

"No problem," I said.

"That's settled," he said. "I don't want to talk about it anymore."

"O.K.," I said. He took the magazine out of my hand. He rolled it up and said, "Whatever you're thinking, stop thinking it."

"I'm not thinking it."

"The doctor does the transfer, not you." He started to get pissed. "Getting worked up" is what we call it in my family, pistols firing off every ten seconds. Watch out, run for cover. He said, "Stop smiling."

"Didn't I mention that I'm a doctor?"

"Shut up, asshole."

"I'm not smiling. I had to yawn. You brought it up, idiot. Not me."

"O.K., forget I said it." I didn't answer him. "How's the article?" He handed the magazine back to me.

"It's O.K. I haven't gotten very far," I said. It was an article about how much money you should give bums. Dave nodded. He didn't care one single shit about quality writing.

We sat there biting the insides of our mouths. Then we said a few more things and went to bed. I didn't feel like going to bed—it was still early—but my brother went around and shut off all the lights in the house. I waited until ten o'clock and phoned Kiff from Dave's office.

She said she was on her way out. I asked her how the bruise on her head was. I whispered, because Dave and Denise were sleeping. She said it had disappeared. She asked me if I was glad to be there. "Yeah," I said. "They're getting a pool."

"That's lovely," she said.

"They have an incredible life here."

"I'm glad," she said, but I could tell by her voice how sad she was. I said, "That was the worst thing I ever did in my life—you know? How can I tell you how sorry I am?"

"It's O.K."

"Anybody else did that to you, I'd kill him."

"Yeah—isn't that funny?" she said.

"No, it's not," I said. "Nothing's funny about it."

"Oh, Vince," she said.

"I'm sorry."

"Me, too."

So it was ten o'clock on Saturday night, and Kiffany was going out. She didn't say where or with who. I didn't ask. It didn't necessarily mean anything. It couldn't be that there was someone else. I'd just seen her a few days earlier. After a minute, thank God, I hung up. My stomach was hurting. I tried to burp, but then I remembered reading that burping was bad for stomach pains.

I went to the kitchen and got some potato chips and took them back to my room and sat there in front of the TV. I was still stuffed from dinner. I ate so many for so long—I don't know how many, it was a big bag—that when I got up to change the channel I was nauseated, and my stomach swung like a watermelon, and the bag was still pretty full. How many potato chips is that—a thousand? A million? The numbers don't do it justice. I felt like I'd eaten sand.

I shut the TV off and got into bed. I fell asleep but after an hour woke up suddenly, not drowsy, wide awake. I felt electrified. I turned the TV back on and thought about my conversation with Dave from before. Sure, it was unlikely—it was a long shot they'd ever need my help. Or would they? Dave smoked a lot of herb in college. Maybe it zapped his supply. Here was my older brother, really scared, and I was his confidant—me, his crummy little brother. What if they did need me? I'd be the father. All of a sudden I was Dave's confidant and possibly a whole lot more. Dave and Denise and me, Uncle Vince, and my semen. I lay there in the guest room, thinking random thoughts, like what if I suddenly went blind in five years.

Would I use a cane or a dog? Would the kid come and see me? Would the state provide me with adequate housing? Medicaid would never pay for a prostitute, but could I find a nurse somewhere to give me hand jobs? Then I came up with a new way to arrange the equipment in the recording studio at work. I could order this special stacking table. There was a bunch of backlog we could dump.

We would be so close, Denise and Dave and me; still, despite my pledge of loyalty to Dave, I would indeed be the father. He took a risk in asking for my help. Maybe one day, when my kid was forty, I'd pull him aside and tell him. "Son," I'd say, "sit down." That would be cool. No, maybe not. Anyhow, I had given my worthless word to do this, because that's what Dave and Denise wanted, and you don't shortchange your family. I wanted to do it. I wanted to help so badly. I was dying to be of service in their embarrassing time of need.

I lay there in the pitch dark, out of breath, practically. I started singing that old Tom Jones thing, "It's not unusual to be loved by anyone." The next line I thought of—"It's not unusual to be drugged by anyone"—came out in this high-pitched voice like a sixth-grader's, so I stopped.

SUNDAY MORNING I got up after ten. I was still tired. Maybe I was tired from oversleeping. My hip was sore from falling on that damned root. My hair was dirty. I thought about showering. I wondered if I'd be able to go

back home after Labor Day and do what I'd been doing before, with Kiffany and work. I couldn't picture it. I sat down and opened the Sunday paper. I thought I was the only one in the house. Then Denise came up from the basement with laundry. She handed me a folded pile of my clothes. She must have picked them up off my floor and washed them. "Wow, thanks," I said.

I asked her where Dave was. She said he had a meeting, and went into the kitchen. I followed her. "Hey, let me help," I said. "Put me to work. I've been sitting on my ass long enough."

She was smiling, but I knew what she thought of me: She thought I was a dope. And she was married to the brother of a dope. She put her apron on. There was flour all over the counter. I sat down on a stool. She tied the apron around the front.

"It's not work," she said. "I like baking."

Denise had her hair down. Her cheeks were smooth, like girls' in high school. Underneath the apron she was wearing a yellow track sweatshirt that had been mine ten years ago. Dave must have stolen it from me. Her boobs came up around the top part of the apron. She looked hot in everything.

I said, "What are you doing?"

"I'm making muffins. I'm about ready to screw this up."

"What kind of muffins?"

"Pumpkin," she said. "I think there's a mistake in the

recipe." She was reading the recipe carefully, rubbing flour around on her hands. She had long fingernails and nail polish. Women claim long fingernails get in the way, but these didn't. From where I sat, I could smell Denise's perfume, or her shampoo, whatever that odor was—Denise's smell. It smelled beautiful. When you're not around them you forget. Man, I was so hard up. I was dying for something. She went to the refrigerator and opened it, and I looked at her sweet ass. She had on running shorts, they were slit on the sides, and the top parts of her thighs were the kind you immediately think about sucking on—firm, yet round and cute. She took out a bowl and dumped some dough on the floury part of the counter.

"Is that for the muffins?"

"No. I'm making bread, too."

She picked up the dough and looked at me. Such blue eyes. It made thinking impossible. I wanted to give my sister-in-law a kiss. On the mouth. Take her into my arms, hold her face, and ram my tongue down her throat. She put her hand up to her head, and when she pulled it away there was flour in her hair.

"What the hell," she said.

"What?"

"What if we can't have kids?"

"Nah," I said. "Your body's not flawed."

Her eyes filled with tears. "I've heard there are doctors who exaggerate to get the most money."

"That's true," I said. "It happens a lot. Don't worry."

She wiped her eyes. "If my uterus is damaged, I might not be able to have a baby."

I nodded. Dave had explained that to me the night before. She said, "See, a woman has a lot of fragile parts inside. There's the vagina, and then there's the cervix, and the uterus—"

"Calm down," I said.

"Jesus Christ," she said.

I said, "Dave thinks it's him."

"It's not him. He's paranoid."

"That's what I told him."

"I've been thinking about this nonstop. I feel like my brain is on fire."

"It's not," I said.

"I lie in bed thinking about it all the time. I feel like I have cancer."

"You don't have cancer," I said.

She cursed again. "Tuesday I go back, and they do it. They tell you right away."

"Uh-huh," I said. She flung the dough around, doing judo on it.

"I'll be so glad when this is over. You know what I mean?"

"Sure, absolutely. Look, Denise, I want to help. I can help."

"You're so generous."

"That's not what I mean," I said.

She said, "Dave and I would have the most beautiful

baby," and all of a sudden she burst into tears. I just sat there with her crying. "We're not really going to be denied this, are we?" she said. Denise looked right at me, her eyes red and swimming. She held her hand out, palm up, as if she was begging for change. I didn't know what she wanted. The whole thing was making me sweaty. Tears dropped off either side of her mouth into flour on the counter.

"No, no way." I hopped off the stool and went to the bathroom for a tissue. I handed it to her.

She said, "I don't care how many we have."

"I know," I said. "You'll have five, you'll have ten." She asked if I was being sincere. I told her Dave was a late bloomer and he'd be interested in intercourse till he's ninety.

I stood beside her and got involved in the baking. I rolled the dough into a ball, put the ball in a pan and the pan in the oven. I suggested she shelve the muffin idea for another time. She wiped her face with her apron. I made a pot of tea, and we sat in the new room and drank it, surrounded by glass walls and plants. Denise's face was puffy. She held a crumpled napkin in her hand. I did imitations of her and Dave yelling: "Denise, where are my damned socks?"—"Gee, I don't know, Dave, they're your socks." Her eyes were bloodshot. Tears poured out and ran down her cheeks when she laughed.

DAVE CAME BACK. He went past us to the sink and got out the bottle of aspirin, without noticing that Denise had been

crying. He said he was going back to bed. We followed him as far as the living room. He threw his briefcase onto the couch and sat down on an antique needlepoint chair. Denise sat near him, on the couch, reaching her hand over both of his.

I said, "How did the meeting go?"

"I don't know."

"Everything's O.K.?" I said.

"It's going good, it's going good. How does somebody gauge that? It's going O.K. to me."

Denise leaned over and kissed his cheek. She combed the back of his hair with her hand. He looked at her and laughed. He wiped his nose. She said, "Did they serve you food or anything?"

"Cookies and iced tea."

I said, "It wasn't a long meeting."

"No. I showed them the new campaign. They bought that." He looked at the coffee table. "What can I say? We met at the brother-in-law's house. He owns a Doberman pinscher. Everything went *tutto bene*. It's going great. Everybody relax."

"O.K.," I said. "Nobody's asking."

"They're boring. Stupid fucking meatballs."

"Uh-huh," I said.

"My neck is sore," he said, and reached back and rubbed it. "It kills me that these people have so much money and I don't."

"We have enough money," Denise said.

"Not like this. It breaks my heart. You wouldn't believe what the family's worth—and they're all morons. The men wear these necklaces. The wives keep getting nose jobs. What a mentality. Did I tell you about their art?"

We said no.

"The brother-in-law's an art collector," he said. "He collects dogs. Anything that has to do with dogs. He's got carved dogs, stuffed dogs, wooden dogs, paintings of dogs. He's even got a dalmatian-covered sofa. It must not be real. Or maybe it is—who knows?" Dave looked at me. I shrugged. He went on. "They have this lamp, and the base of the lamp is a dog pissing on a fire hydrant, and a boy squatting next to it." I laughed. He said, "I hate working for these guys."

Denise kissed the back of Dave's hand. "I'm sorry," she said.

He said, "You know what I do? My secret for success with them? I throw away my intelligent ideas. I don't even bother showing them, and I write the corniest crap I can think up. We're doing a promotion with the muffler chain, so this morning I said, 'Instead of calling it a sale, let's call it a carnival.' It was the most idiotic thing I could think of. I said, 'We'll decorate our stores like the Mardi Gras.' So Carlo calls the Meathead and the grandma in and we all have a Sambuca at nine o'clock in the morning." Dave laughed.

I said, "Sambuca?"

"He needed help with the concept. The grandmother

doesn't even fucking speak English. She's from Romania or someplace."

Dave leaned back, laughing, stretching with his hands over his head. His baseball hat fell off, backward. He'd become almost bald, and his hair was all stuck down. "What's an eighty-year-old grandma gonna know about mufflers?" he said. He was giggling in a high-pitched voice. His eyes teared, and he smeared them with his fingers. He stretched, sticking his chest out, and the needlepoint chair he sat on creaked, and then a noise came from underneath it—a screech like wood being pulled apart. He sat forward. He said, "Shit—am I breaking this chair?"

Denise smiled, but she didn't move.

He said, "Has it always wobbled like this?" He shook it.

Denise said, "It's very old. It's not worth anything."

"I've got to get away from those guys," he said. He rubbed his head. "They're destroying my brain." I nodded, listening to him rave. "I hate this kind of work," he said. "What a waste of a year."

My tea had cooled then, so I drank it. "It sounds like you want to quit," I said. He looked up at me. "So why don't you quit and stop crying?"

"Oh, fuck you."

"O.K. Sorry, forget it," I said.

"I can't quit," Dave said. He stood up and took a tissue out of his pocket. He unfolded it and blew his nose. I watched him. He had no energy. Outside I heard a lawn mower running somewhere.

"Ah, Vinny," he said, and sat down again. The chair creaked again. It sounded like a bird squawking. He kept looking at me.

"What?" I said.

"Little Vinchi," he said. I didn't say anything. "Isn't that what I used to call you?"

"Don't call me that."

"O.K., whatever. Don't get excited. What happened to my hat?"

Denise leaned over and kissed his biceps. "It's behind you," she said.

Dave crumpled the tissue up and threw it over his shoulder onto the floor.

WE HAD A last, quiet dinner that night, of all the tasty left-overs. Monday morning I packed up. On my way out, I saw they had wheeled one of those beautiful new chaises to the front of the house. Dave said it was mine. I don't know what I did to deserve it. He helped me strap it to the roof of my car. He said they didn't need six. I put the cushions in the trunk, careful not to get any dirt on them. Of everything I owned, this would be my nicest possession. Then we all said good-bye in the driveway.

I cruised up the Garden State Parkway. It was sunny and hot out, with that beautiful chair above me, shuddering in the wind. I kept looking up to make sure it was still there. When I got home, I put the new chair in my apartment, next to a table with a plant on it. Then I sat down and

wrote my brother a note. The chair was the most beautiful thing I'd ever seen, and I said so. I thought of them, down there, going to the doctors. At last, after all these years, I knew more about Dave than I wanted to.

KIFFANY AND I finally broke up permanently. When I think about it now, it seems normal to be away from her, but I haven't stopped loving her yet, and that's a pain in the ass. Probably the best thing to do is scope out somebody else, and try to make it different this time. I've walked by Kiffany's every day, to and from work. I've seen guys' cars in her driveway, and I've thought about going over there with a real gun—maybe I'd put on camouflage face paint and boots, some cologne for effect, walk right in there and shoot them in the middle of their beaujolais. But what's that? Definitely not love in a derivative form.

At work we stayed away from each other, and then, a few months ago, her whole department moved across the street. It's over now between us, and that's the best anybody can hope for.

THE ROYAL PALMS

LAST WINTER, WE went on vacation to the Caribbean. When the plane landed, we were so exhausted we could barely lift our bags. We checked in at the hotel, and got rid of the suitcases, and without unpacking went out the gate to look at the casino. A guard pointed us in the opposite direction from the beach, down a lonely dirt road, a five-minute walk from the hotel gate.

The casino was a small white stucco building, with bars on the windows and a brown wooden sign. There were some German tourists in there, and I overheard a couple of Americans talking, but the rest of the faces in the room were either friendly employees or locals—whatever, black people, people from there. I played blackjack, and I was on a roll. Winning relaxes me; at some point in the night I was up two thousand dollars. Diane played the slot machines, going all night without a hit, waiting for me to finish. I

cashed out because the place was closing. It was just after one in the morning. We were practically the last ones in there, definitely the last white ones in the place. They paid out my winnings and I followed Diane to the door.

I had a buzz on. I put the money in the belly of my shirt, because I couldn't carry it all in my pockets. It was half the cost of the trip, although that wasn't an issue. Two guys came out of the casino behind us, local guys, and we nodded to them and they went to their car. They pulled it around in our direction. Diane looked back and saw the car; she looked at me—there was that funny moment—and then she started running down the road.

The car came up behind us. It took me a second to figure out what was going on. Diane had a ten- or twenty-yard lead on me—she's a fast runner, she was a gymnast in high school—and I started running with all this goddamn money bouncing around, but I couldn't keep up. I was telling her to wait for me, and yelling at her not to run, because it would only make things worse, incriminate us or attract their attention, although she did have a point. The car kept slowing down, because the road was in terrible shape. I was running as fast as possible, Diane's white pants disappearing in the dark in front of me, the money bouncing around everywhere in my shirt. Lights from the hotel loomed in front of us now, the car bounding into those barrel-size humps and potholes, its headlights leaping across us and up into the trees. I could hear the thumping of the engine—it was an old jeep and it sounded like a

washing machine—but the noise came both from right be-
hind me and from far away, echoing through the woods. I
was chugging now, gaining on Diane. I could see the hotel
guard, asleep in his shack.

We got to the gate and the guard sat up. The car pulled
up alongside us, and the two guys looked over at us, and we
looked at them. The guard had a shotgun. He went and
spoke to the driver. Then they turned around and drove
away. I had been happy back there at the blackjack table,
beating the slit-eyed dealer, but with the sudden heat and
the run down the road, the airplane food and the funny
smell of this fertile jungle, I wanted to puke.

We were staying in a bungalow beside the main build-
ing, one of a row of cottages in the trees along the beach.
Diane went into the bathroom without a word. I was so
freaked that I didn't know what to do. I didn't want that
cash in there with us, so after she went to sleep I walked
around back, behind the cabin, and buried the money in
the sand. It was dark.

Then I got into bed. I listened to Diane breathe. I
couldn't tell if she was asleep or not, and I'd become afraid
of that lately, of not knowing—and of how it didn't matter.
We hadn't had sex since Thanksgiving. Diane said her ass
was too fat. We hadn't enjoyed each other's company now
in a long time, and before this trip there were nights when
we didn't speak. Earlier that day, standing in line at the air-
port with all our luggage, she said to me, "I'm fat. I feel
ugly."

I said, "We're going on a great vacation, so try to have fun."

She said, "You hate me." I didn't know what to say. I did hate her, partly, she was right, but not for being fat: Diane is small and cute, everything on her is round and full anyway. But I was taking it very seriously that she was repulsed by me, that she stopped me anytime I tried to touch her.

I still felt love for her, too, but we didn't have the same outlook anymore. And I didn't like listening to her complain all the time. My life was going the way I always thought it should—I mean my job, and money. The contracts I'd sold last quarter were huge, my company had just bought a smaller firm and merged, we were booming—and I had nobody to tell that to. Diane's job was a total disappointment, or so she claimed, though she could never be specific. She mentioned getting a master's in something, or learning to make jewelry, but that might be too complicated. At home, she ate frozen Snickers bars in bed. She made Kool-Aid every night and chugged it from the pitcher. I hadn't seen Diane in her underwear in months, or her bare shoulders or her pretty chest, or her pale, round thighs; she said she was flab, pure Jell-O; she said her potbelly hung over the waist of her skirt. At night she'd put on her big purple sweatshirt that came down to her knees; she'd pull the hood up over her head and tie the string and get into bed and turn off the lights. It got so messed up that I couldn't even kiss her—she'd laugh or cover her lips and say, "I have to wax my mustache." We had more money

now, and sometimes we discussed doing something new, either kids or a new house; neither one felt like the natural thing, but what were we going to do next? Something was missing. We needed the next phase, and we needed what was missing to get to the next phase. I didn't know whether to be worried or not.

THE NEXT MORNING I went out to get the money I'd buried in the sand. As I was digging, I saw it all again in my mind, the banged-up jeep turning and then Diane running. Who knows what those guys wanted—they probably thought we were crazy—but it occurred to me then that she'd never looked back. What if I'd tripped? Maybe I missed something, but I felt terrible then, remembering: Diane, running away from me. The money was all wet; I'd packed it in a plastic bag, and a jogger who walked by wondered if it was shellfish I had caught.

I had the hotel clerk change it into big bills and put it in the vault. He assured me that nothing bad had ever happened here, and never would, that I was perfectly safe. The natives were friendly, he said; I should forget it and begin to enjoy myself.

The food area was a vast tented pavilion, with plush, oversized chairs and an enormous breakfast buffet of all different kinds of exotic food. I had the cook make me an omelette. He was dark black, like the guys from the night before. I looked over at Diane, who had a couple of orange slices and a banana on her plate. I said, "Hey, come on, eat

something. We're on vacation." She said she didn't want to get too full.

As we walked to the water, I said I liked her new straw hat. She said, "If you stare at my gut I will kill you."

I rubbed some sunscreen on. The beach was totally empty. Where the hell was everybody? "Jesus Christ," I said to Diane, "this is some fucking resort."

At lunch the place was full, though, and then the crowd came to the beach, and later that afternoon there was a softball game and we joined in. I got a hit that went over the shortstop's head. Diane pitched for the other team and somehow lobbed strikes. That evening we ate pasta and shellfish. They had drummers in the pavilion, but we were too tired to stay for more than a minute, and I slept that night the way you'd hope to sleep on vacation—like a five-year-old kid with no troubles. I dreamed about my base hit and woke up to birds singing outside the window. We had pancakes for breakfast, and later the staff organized a big tug-of-war and a sack race, and we met some more of the other guests. Our team won the sack race but lost the tug-of-war.

WE CLAIMED A spot for ourselves on the beach. Every morning you could find us there. We spent our day swimming, napping, baking in the sun. After a couple of days your eyes don't fight the landscape. The beach was gorgeous; it started at the dock and wound along for half a mile, narrow in some places, funneling into a rocky

point with a jetty. The ocean was blue—deep, brilliant turquoise—except that at noon, with the sun directly overhead, it turned the color of tin. Low tide left lumps of seaweed like piles of old, wet wigs; guys came by with rakes and took them away. On the rim of the beach there were big palm trees to lie under. It was cool in the shade. If you waved to one of the staff guys, he'd bring you a chaise.

We got used to it. I figured out how you adjust your chaise without chopping off a finger. Where to go to eat lunch, which way to the Tiki Bar. I found a shortcut through the pricker bushes to the cottage. It's a resort, so it's yours as much as it is anybody's. You know some other people now, so you say hello. I sat there staring at the water and thought back to my life: breakfast meetings, angry clients, me in a rage at the office, somebody crying, somebody quitting, me driving back home wondering what kind of mood we'll both be in that night—days come in like the surf, and I'm sand, I'm the rocks, and it pounds me.

Diane bought a flowered bikini in the hotel store. She looked floral in it, but she wrapped a towel around her waist whenever she stood up. Her hair looked shiny in the sun. Her skin was getting darker. Then the sun would go behind a cloud, she'd tuck her hair behind her ear and turn a page, the wind would come up off the ocean—and I'd see her nipples through the fabric of her bathing suit and I'd have to look away. Her body was soft, round peaches. I'd think, Don't rush it. You'll make a fool of yourself. I wondered what the hell we were going to do.

．　　　．　　　．

WE WERE HAVING lunch one day under the big top, and this couple came up and introduced themselves. Their names were Rick and Joanie. They had just got there the night before and were staying in the bungalow right next to ours, it turned out. Our table was empty, and we invited them to sit. He was an outdoor-type guy, tall and athletic, with a mustache—he had on a black tank top, with smooth, flat muscles underneath it—and she was tall and fit with sandy blond hair, like him. They were already tan. They hadn't got their plates yet, so we told them what the better dishes were on the buffet and what to steer clear of, and what they run out of every day, and like that.

Rick said, "Have you tried the goatfish?" He told us the fish was a delicacy here. When they came back with food, they had some of that fish on their plates and brought an extra piece for us to try.

They lived in northern Florida. Joanie was an actress. She said she did a lot of local television commercials. She had huge teeth and a big, wide smile. When we stood up, later, I realized she was about a foot taller than me. Rick sold powerboats; he had two dealerships and a third one on the way. He had broad shoulders and big hands, a thin nose and smooth skin, and a steel diving watch on his left wrist. I'm not that tall, or as good-looking as some guys, but I'm not an ugly fucking freak or anything. These two were perfect, though. They looked like models, big models who lifted weights. They had a boy, five, and a girl, two, and they

showed us pictures of them, and Rick had a picture of himself on his Harley, giving the thumbs-up. I said they must still be exhausted from the flight, but Rick pulled his hair back in a rubber band and said he'd already reserved a court for paddle tennis later.

He asked me what I thought of the fish. I said it was good. Rick said they really knew how to cook it here; it tasted like butter.

THE NEXT MORNING I was walking down the beach and I saw Rick. He said, "Hey, neighbor, where you going?"

I said, "Nowhere," and Rick said, "I'm going fishing. Come on." I'd never been fishing. I ran back to our suite. Diane was taking a nap. I didn't know what to bring. I grabbed my Swiss Army knife and left a note: "Didn't want to wake you up, honey—Rick and I went fishing."

The resort chartered a boat twice a week to take people out, and besides us there were seven or eight other guests on board. It headed toward the horizon, loud and stinking of diesel fuel. Then they shut the engine off and everybody dropped their lines. It was amazing out there. Rick fished. I didn't fish. I watched the other people.

I saw a couple of sailboats and some birds—it was quiet this far from shore—and if you stared over the side into the water you could make out the bottom, thirty or forty feet down. Rick kept taking things out of his pockets: a piece of gum, a chunk of bait, a pill from a bottle of medicine, a visor, a box of Tic-Tacs. He put on sunscreen and smoothed

his mustache. Then his rod snagged—it was so bent I thought he would snap it—and he pulled a fish right out of the water, a beautiful, flat, wide fish, shimmering aquamarine color. It had incredible skin. He held it up; it was flipping around like crazy. I'd never seen a fish like that. I wasn't sure if he wanted to keep it or throw it back, but he laid it on the deck and stepped on it and stuck a knife into its head. Then he threw it in a Ziploc bag.

"That, right there," he said, "is good eating." I watched as the interior of the bag fogged over with moisture. I think the fish was still moving.

I said, "Is it dead?"

He said, "What do you mean?"

"Would you kill it, please?"

He said, "It's dead."

"Is that goatfish?"

"That? No."

WE HAD BEERS from a cooler and watched the other people fish. There was a woman across from us wearing a thing like a black slip and drinking a Coke. Rick said, "Look at her. She's incredible. My dick's been hard the whole day."

She looked like *Breakfast at Tiffany's*—that actress with the skinny neck. I smiled at her. She smiled back. "Guess what," Rick said. "She wants to fuck you." They started the engine again, and we cruised along the water, spray coming over the side and hitting us. He kept staring at the woman. She flipped her long black hair, talking with the captain,

and turned her beautiful ass in our direction. She was small and had a girl's waist and tan shoulders. Her legs were perfect. He said, "What I'd do to get my rocket off in her." The boat was turning around then. We headed back.

They let us out at the dock, a short way from the buildings and the people lying out on the sand. We came walking up the beach with Rick's fish, and Rick went someplace to clean it. The women, Joanie and Diane, were lying side by side.

"Look at this," Diane said, and sat up to show me the back of her head. "Joanie did this to my hair." It was all braided in teeny rows. She was excited.

"That's wild, honey," I said. "Thanks, Joanie."

She said, "No problem." She was propped up on her elbow, with her free hand covering her eyes like a visor. She squinted into the sun, smiling hopefully.

"Here," I said, and tossed her my baseball hat.

"Thanks," she said, and pulled it down and swung her ponytail out the back. I looked at Diane—her mouth was hanging open in surprise. Did she want my hat for herself? I guess so.

She slid down to wipe the sand off her feet, and I knelt beside her and kissed her. I took her hand and held it. I ducked down and kissed her neck. She giggled and said to Joanie, "Maybe I should get my ears pierced." Joanie was staring down the beach looking for her husband. She was already very tan and had a swimmer's body—taut, trim, and lanky; she had beautiful bosoms, and her hipbones jutted

up so nicely you could've hung Christmas ornaments on them. I kissed Diane's throat and held her thin braids in my hand. She jerked her head away. "My hair's filthy," she said. Joanie looked down the blanket at us, over the delicate arch of her pelvis, and smiled.

THE FOUR OF us sat together at dinner that night and drank wine. I ate this fish stew in a flaky pie crust, and after dinner the staff built a bonfire on the beach and we took another bottle of wine and went down there.

They'd dragged big logs over for us to sit on, and I sat down next to the guy stoking the fire. It was chilly out. The fire was heating up one side of my face, making it swell, and the sea breeze hit me on the other side and it felt numb. The local guys were talking to each other a mile a minute— it was totally unintelligible—and across the circle I saw Diane chatting with a couple we'd met on the airport van.

Our vacation was half over. On the whole, things were better. Was that what Diane thought, too? Or had she stopped loving me, and couldn't say so? I kept wondering if this was the end. I was sitting in a jolly crowd of people. I sipped my wine. Rick was standing over on the side, talking with the woman from the boat; he opened her beer for her with a thing on his key chain and took a swig. The girl laughed. Joanie was two feet away from them. She still had that dopey smile plastered on her face. She sat Indian style on the sand, looking tan and tired, watching the fire.

After a minute, Rick sat down. He was wearing white

tennis shorts and a flannel shirt with the sleeves ripped off, and I thought, What kind of guy brings a ripped shirt with him on vacation? It was cold out, and everybody else was wearing jackets. He didn't seem cold. The fire glowed in his golden hair. He had dimples next to his mouth, and he wore his hair long and curly. He moved down the log right next to me. He was tan as hell, his arm muscles were like knotted brown wood. Rick had the looks—handsome and strong and cool at the same time, that was him. Like those guys you knew in high school who had it all. He probably used to drive a Camaro with a surfboard on it.

On the other side of the circle there were two hotel guys playing guitars. They weren't spectacular or terrible, but one guy had a nice voice. Rick asked me how everything was; we talked about home, how it seemed like a million miles away. I started to tell him about my problems, my crummy sex life with Diane. I don't know why—people do funny things on vacation.

He listened, staring into the fire. I tried to keep the descriptions as vague as possible, and then I thought, fuck it—some stupid boat dealer from the Everglades who I'm never gonna see again, so what if he knows my wife has a mustache? He said he understood. He was, it turned out, totally cool. We talked about how married people get along together. He rubbed his chin. "That's all normal," he said. "You have to work around it."

So, as Diane and I walked back to our suite, I grabbed some matches and asked for a candle from the front desk.

Following Rick's advice, I gave Diane a neck rub, and put some warm water in a bowl and got a washcloth. I washed her neck and shoulders with the cloth. She asked me what I was doing, and I told her to be quiet. I washed her hands and her fingers; I untied her sandals and washed the tops of her feet. She said, "That feels good." I put some lotion on her elbows. She let me undress her. I took her shirt off, and her bra; I undid her shorts and pulled them off. She lay down and smiled, and I took the cloth and rubbed it in slow circles over her entire body.

I loved her, I still knew that. This was my princess here. We weren't going to die from this. I sat beside her, and we talked about the trip so far, the dinners, the bonfire, those guys in the jeep who were trying to kill us. She'd signed up for a windsurfing lesson for later in the week and was all excited about going. I put some moisturizer on her shoulders and brushed her hair, and then I took all my clothes off and lay there next to her. We seemed happy. She was cute as hell. In the past four days, the sun had made her hair lighter. Her arms and legs were dark, her tummy was a lighter shade of tan; where the bikini had been was pure white. I mentioned a few things about life at home, how we needed to make some changes, to plan for the future. Diane had her arm under her head, and every few minutes she shut her eyes. Her eyelids were almost white against her tan face. When I asked her if she was sleepy she said no. We stayed like that for a while.

It reminded me of a scene out of high school—the candle on the table, both of us buzzed on wine, my dick wanging around between us. I looked down the length of her body and put my hand on her. She didn't move. I was thinking the way I had in high school, too—like I would do anything just to touch her. She yawned. I pictured doing it to her even if she passed out. Diane said, "Excuse me." I was dying to fuck my wife. I was sizzling. As soon as I tried something—I moved myself against her and put my lips on her neck—she jumped back and a look crossed her face; she said my beard was scratchy. And then she started talking a mile a minute about the woman in the cabin next to Joanie's who'd seen an iguana, how it ran across her foot and disappeared into the woods, and we lay there, nobody saying a word now. In a few more minutes, I heard her breathing change. The candle was still going, flickering alongside us. She'd fallen asleep.

THE NEXT DAY, as we were eating our jambalaya for lunch, they came by. Joanie asked Diane if she wanted to go shopping. Diane said yes, and Rick said he'd rented a mountain bike and heard of some trails that went up into the hills, if I was interested. I didn't feel like it, and with everybody gone I went into our room and called my office. I turned on my computer and faxed them some stuff, and spent an hour on the phone with our comptroller—we'd had a scare with a big supplier, but it was O.K. now. I

returned some other calls. Everything was fine. At four o'clock, I looked up. The day was ending. There were three days left of our vacation, it had flown by, and what the fuck was I doing crapping around inside?

I walked toward the hotel's plaza, feeling pale and tired. My hands were sweaty. I hated myself for missing the sun, and now the ocean was calm and the breeze had died. Salt covered everything—stones, leaves, the spotlights sticking up every five feet in the ground. I walked back and forth between the tennis courts and the place where we usually sat on the beach. There were some European-looking dudes in our spot, wearing skimpy Speedos; I felt like walking up to them and kicking in their skulls. I didn't see anyone I knew, as if a whole crew of fresh guests, all ghostly white and uncomfortable, had come in the night before and replaced the old ones. A woman stood next to me with her baby, changing its diaper in the middle of the plaza, stinking up the joint with her kid's smelly dump. When I finally saw a familiar face go by—the kitchen-staff guy who made my omelettes—I was so relieved I almost hugged him. He was carrying a three-foot-long fish—a tuna, he said, seventy pounds; it had just come off a boat. I followed him to an outdoor kitchen, and while he cut it up I asked him about growing up on the island.

Later I was sitting in the hotel lobby, reading the newspaper, when Rick came in with his bicycle. He had on tight black bicycle-rider pants, and his thick, muscular legs were

all tan and defined, with big veins on his calves. He said the ride had been "killer," and showed me on a map where he'd gone. Then he pulled me up by the arm with his iron grip and yanked off his sunglasses—he had a raccoon stripe of white where the glasses had been. Talking low, he told me there were guys out there living forty feet up in the trees, pot growers with machine guns who almost shot him but then took him in and befriended him. He said they were the most amiable guys, and he talked with them and smoked pot and sang reggae. They gave him a tour of their jungle hideout. They'd made crude musical instruments out of tin boxes and wire, and they had their feet propped up on crates of ammo. He said, "One of them went to Oxford."

I said, "Congratulations."

He said, "They ship the pot out in these carved heads, the dark wood carving this area is known for, called *obiko*. Joanie was supposed to buy one when she went into town today. They stuff the shit into a hollowed-out part of the heads and ship them around the world."

I said, "Is that so?"

Rick said, "Listen, come back up with me tomorrow. You can't believe the view."

I said, "Not in a million years."

"I'm taking Joanie," he said.

"You're not taking Joanie up there. They'll gang-rape her."

"They're the friendliest people in the world. They gave

me dope. They had piles of it lying around." He started to reach into his bicycle pants, in the middle of the lobby. He said, "I got it here somewhere."

"Rick—what the fuck are you doing?" I said, and grabbed his hand.

He said, "Possession of marijuana is not a crime here. And even if it is, they want the tourists to smoke it."

DIANE ASKED RICK to tell the whole story again at dinner. I was sick of it and said nothing. I was going gambling again at that little shack. It was "casino night," whatever that meant. Rick came with me. I agreed on the condition that he leave his wacky weed at home. Diane stayed with Joanie. There was a lounge singer in the nightclub, and they went to see his act.

The casino was busier that night. There were lines for the slot machines and a crowd at every table. I played blackjack. I ate about a thousand pounds of salty cashews and didn't drink. Rick stood next to me, and after an hour a seat opened up at the table and he decided to play.

"I'll be your wingman," he said, stacking his chips in ten-dollar piles.

Blackjack is pretty simple: You need some luck, you need to be able to add up to twenty-one, and like that. I've seen all kinds of systems, basic card counting, charts guys carry with statistical analysis; I've seen guys with backers—professionals—and I've seen people asked to leave casinos for various offenses. Rick bet erratically, in no particular

pattern; I couldn't tell if he had any experience at all, and I watched him rip through his bank and go back to the cashier for more chips. He talked to himself and filled up on vodka, and when his bank was gone he went back another time. I couldn't bear to look. He bummed a cigarette off somebody and mentioned going water-skiing in the morning, and told me how he gave up smoking, cold turkey, on New Year's Day. "This is my first puff in a month," he said.

I said, "If you get rid of that hand, you might not lose as fast." He ignored me.

Meanwhile, I did well. I'm good at math, and blackjack is a lot of math. At one point, the dealer aimed his finger at me and said, "You're tough," and I shrugged. I felt like David Hasselhoff. I pointed back at him and then didn't say a word except when I needed a card. Rick was out, he'd played like an imbecile, and he stayed to watch me, hunched over in his skintight rugby shirt.

I took a card. The dealer busted. I watched all the hopeful people around me losing money, and then a new dealer took over, and I cashed in almost nine hundred bucks. I won, and the house lost. As we walked back to the hotel—it wasn't even midnight, and it was cool and breezy like every other night since I'd arrived—Rick asked me to give him his money back. It was five hundred dollars. He said, "Please, buddy." I tried to tell him that the money he lost was no longer his money—it was the bank's—and what I had was different money, not his. He started explaining:

He said he'd been drunk, the rules were different here from the ones in the casino he played in, whatever. I said to him, "Why don't you go for a swim?" He said no. He begged me. I started laughing and pretended to play the violin. He told me Joanie had refused to let him take money for gambling, but he'd taken it anyway, and now he'd blown it, and he needed the money before we got back or she'd kill him. I said no. He asked me one more time. "What do I look like?" I said. "Get an advance on your credit card."

We got to Rick and Joanie's cabin. I could hear the women inside. I said to him, "Next time you gamble you need to have a figure in your head, a top amount you can lose," but he told me to shut up. Then he opened the door, and we went inside.

The women said the lounge singer was a Caribbean man named Mr. High-Five, and started dancing around the bed. Diane had ordered two pizzas from room service, and there was food all over the place. Rick sat in a chair in the corner with his hat on backward. He looked fried, as if he got a sunburn on the bike that day. Diane and I went to our room.

We were in bed with the lights off when Rick knocked at the door. I went outside and stood on the paved path with him. The moon was shining on the water. He'd been crying. I could see where the discussion was about to go. He wore wrinkled blue boxers and white socks. He'd taken his hat off, and I noticed he had hives on his forehead, probably from riding his bike through the jungle.

He said he felt like crap inside. He said he loved me, he told me he was so surprised to find a friend at one of these places that he couldn't believe his luck. "You know what I mean?" he said. I saw that the light was on in their room, which meant Joanie probably knew he'd lost the money. He was talking about the fish we'd caught together. "There's nothing like fishing with your friend," he said. His oratory didn't seem to be rounding any corner. There were so many different stupid things about this moment, now he was telling me how he got ripped off buying some Kruger-rands, I wanted him to shut the fuck up, I didn't know what to do, I went back into my bungalow and got five hundred dollars from the night's winnings and handed it to him. I said, "Here."

He said, "Thank you."

I didn't answer him. I thought he was full of shit.

He went back in and shut the door. I stood there, out-side my doorway, furious at myself. His light went off. I dis-tinctly heard him say something to Joanie. I waited another minute. I didn't hear anything else.

My watch said 2 A.M. A mosquito came up and bit my eyelid, but I didn't feel like going inside yet. I was sweating. Right next door, if I needed them, were my new friend Rick and his piece-of-ass wife. And in my bungalow I had my own no-fuck, don't-touch wife sleeping off her pizza pies. I had a view of the ocean, the seaborne air, mountains in back of me, jungles full of tree-climbing pot freaks. In the moonlight, there were swans or storks,

maybe pelicans, gliding above the calm sea, looking for a fish to spear.

THE NEXT DAY'S weather was like all the others. Diane and I swam and read our books and lay on the beach. Joanie appeared at lunch and joined us; she looked tired, and the three of us said almost nothing as we ate. I asked about Rick, and she shrugged, and from then on we baked in the sun, watching the water. Joanie told us she'd talked to her kids that morning; their grandpa had made them spaghetti sandwiches, and they loved it. We swam, and later Joanie said Rick was probably playing tennis, and at dinner, when we still didn't see him, she said he was exhausted and had never woken up from his nap.

We said good night and went to bed. This time it was Diane who started up. She kissed me and I kissed her back. I held her tits. She opened my shorts and massaged me with a feathery touch of her fingertips, kind of teasing.

It went on for, I don't know, a while. There was all this circling, circling—had she forgotten how to do everything? She was doing a terrible job. I couldn't stand it anymore, I shoved her out of the way and started rubbing myself. It was not a scene I'd recommend—not loving, if you know what I mean, not the expression of the subtle union between two people. And then Diane started to cry. She said she felt like a failure in every way—I was ready to agree—and then she went the other way and said I didn't know her anymore, that I'd forgotten how it used to be when we

were crazy about each other, that now I didn't give a fuck about anything but making money. She cried and I held her. I regretted whacking off like that, I admitted it made everything worse. But I didn't really care. Without any more fighting, we both fell asleep.

FIRST THING FRIDAY morning, Diane went off to that windsurfing lesson in the bay. Joanie and I sat on the beach and talked. There was still no sign of Rick.

I told her about my business. She said it sounded fascinating. She told me there was a soap opera based in Miami that she was thinking of trying out for. We went swimming. I blew bubbles out my nose, and it cracked her up. Breakfast ended at eleven, and neither of us did anything about it. Eventually I got up and bought us apples at the commissary.

Rick showed up around noon, all sweaty in a tennis outfit and a purple baseball hat with the name of the resort stitched across it. I'd actually missed having him around. Rick's eyes were so green they almost glowed, from all that time in the sun. He was grinning again. Joanie asked if he was hungry; he said no. He had a white plastic bucket and a fishing rod; he went over near the dock and began surf casting.

Joanie was looking at me. I didn't know what she meant. I said, "What are you smiling for?"

She said, "I'm such a fucking idiot."

Diane came back. She was all excited. She sat in the

sand and told us how she got the Windsurfer going—it was tricky—and how the instructor, Philippe, and she and two others went way out into the ocean. She said she'd never had so much fun in her life. The group had had to turn back because the weather was starting to change, but not before they spotted a giant sea turtle, swimming alongside them. She said, "It was huge and gray—it had slimy bumps on its back." I looked off to the horizon, but I couldn't see anything, just a few clouds in a long line above the water.

Diane jumped up to go say hello to Rick over by the dock. They started chatting, and soon she was holding the rod and Rick was leaning around her, showing her how to draw it back with his long, bronze muscles. Rick was tall and broad-shouldered, and Diane was looking up at him. You could hear them laugh. Joanie sat beside me, blinking into the hazy sun, her lips coated in a thick film of sunblock. After a few minutes I laid my head down, and when I looked up Diane and Rick were gone. I took my shirt off and fell asleep.

I woke up to the wind kicking sand, just the way Philippe had said. My mouth was dry. The sun was gone.

The beach was empty. I sat up, my face mashed into wrinkles from the towel. Joanie had passed out, too, curled up beside me in her bikini bottoms and my gray T-shirt. I sat back and looked at her small pink feet, the calluses on her heels and toes, her smooth, hairless thighs, the faint hint of veins beneath the skin. The stretched back of her

red bikini bottoms across her dynamite ass. It was so pretty I wanted to cry. She yawned, reaching her long, thin arms up, and I saw her bikini top lying next to her on the towel.

Joanie sat up on her knees, beside me. "Where did they go?" she said. I didn't know. She'd knotted my shirt so it rode high up on her rib cage. I reached across and pulled the knot. She watched me. My hand slipped underneath the T-shirt, and I felt my palm across her stomach. There was sand stuck on her leg, and I watched her braless boobs moving against the inside of my shirt. I saw her swallow. I felt her breathe.

Diane came walking up the beach from the direction of the jetty. She said she was tired, and did I want to come take a nap with her. A second later we were walking down the beach to our room. Joanie didn't have time to respond.

Diane closed the blinds. I sat down and untied my sneakers. She stepped between my legs and put her tongue against my teeth. She knelt, and yanked off my bathing suit and flung it on the lampshade. I was so excited I started to shake. I sat back on the bed, flustered. She took off her bottoms, standing in front of me, and kissed my throat. I kept looking for marks on her from Rick—a sign of use on my wife's body—but I was so turned on after all this time that I was seeing spots. The place where her bikini had been was glowing. She held my head. I rubbed my face against her stomach.

We lay down and started to do it. She seemed fine, I guess. She was digging it. It was the same old Diane. I held

her sweet face. She said, "It's nice to see you smile again."
Finally, we were grooving.

When it was over, I went into the bathroom and got a
glass of water. My groin was raw. She lay on her stomach,
breathing.

I sat beside her and rubbed my hand across the top of
her ass, as fine as silk.

She said, "I can't move."

"So don't."

"You're the best lover in the world," she said, and
turned over and held me. "I promised Rick I'd go fishing,
on that boat you guys went on." She looked at me. "Is it all
right if I try it? It's our last day."

I said, "Absolutely." She squeezed my body. I hugged
her back, as hard as she was hugging me.

"You feel so good," she said, and I said, "Um-hmm."
The next second she was standing on one leg, trying to get
into her panties. She said, "Thank you."

"For what?"

"For being so wonderful to me."

"No problem," I said. She ran around the room, looking
for clothes. She took my baseball hat and fitted it on her
head. I was still in bed. She leaned down next to me.

"You're the kind of husband women wish for." She gave
me a kiss, pulling my lips with her teeth.

"O.K.," I said. She took the camera and flew out the
door.

. . .

IT WAS FOUR o'clock. I was on my own. I thought of going back to find Joanie on the beach. I flipped open my briefcase and then shut it, and got up and showered and left the bungalow.

I stopped by the Tiki Bar for a last drink. Jimmy, the bartender, was there, washing the bar off with a hose. The woman from the boat came, and we said hello. I hadn't seen her since the bonfire that night.

She was wearing a bikini and had a slim leather belly bag clipped around her waist. She wiggled her ass onto the next bar stool and lit a smoke and said, "Jim, what do I want?" He shoveled ice into the sink, waiting for her to answer. She said, "Rum-and-Coke, my favorite."

"I'm going back to Baltimore on Sunday. I miss my cats," she told me. She'd been here at least a week. She said, "They bill this place as a singles' resort, but I didn't see any singles here. Just me. And a couple of Swedish guys in G-strings."

I said, "How many cats?"

"Two. They're probably dead by now. My sister's been feeding them."

I was thinking about Diane. The perfume smell of her hair, the velvet softness of her baby skin. We got so close. She was floating all around me.

"I bet they're O.K.," I said. "Don't get depressed."

"I'm sick of this Tiki Bar," the woman said. I thought about Diane and Rick—what was she doing? I pictured them fishing and talking and doing whatever else you do on

a boat. Diane and I were in some new place together, and I thought of how it had to keep being new, or else we were doomed. More people came. Here I was, sitting around, depressed. That's because you are a loser, I said to myself. I sipped my daiquiri. It tasted like ice cream. The woman from Baltimore was staring at me. She tapped her cigarette, waiting for me to say something else. I had nothing to say. I stared out at the water as the time passed in long sips. Out beyond the beach, I saw the cruiser pulling back into the harbor.

I said, "Hey—you like lawyers?" She asked why. "My cousin Walt is a lawyer. He's good-looking. He lives in Baltimore."

She said, "Really?"

"He has his own firm. He's loaded."

"Wow."

Walt had a lisp. He talked like Popeye. But he also had muscles and owned a house on two acres in the suburbs.

"Walt's a great guy," I said. "He'd love you." She smiled and put out her cigarette. "I'll call him when we get back."

She gave me a business card from her belly bag. "Something to look forward to," she said.

Diane and Rick came back. They'd seen dolphins, they said. Diane looked beautiful. I wanted to hold her and touch her again. Rick had caught three fish. He was carrying them in a cooler filled with ice. The long one he called a "dagger fish." He didn't know its real name. His jaw was cocked in a big smile. I stared at his straw-colored curls.

Diane sure seemed happy now. What had happened? I didn't have a clue. I thought of all the different combinations. I didn't panic—why the fuck should you panic? While I'm thinking this, though, Rick winked at the barstool next to me, at the woman, and she smiled and blushed. Diane looked at me and I looked at her and Rick. I still haven't figured out what was going on. He showed me the other two fish; he wanted to take them home in dry ice and smoke them, and send them to me in the mail. I said, "I do not accept dead fish in the mail," and finished my drink. Diane came over and grabbed me. I put my arm around her and held her tight. The cook ended up broiling the fish for dinner. Rick bought all the wine.

"Here's to us," he said, "and fuck the mortgage." He was all smiles, and our happiness continued. Later in the evening, I found out they were a lot more than that five hundred dollars behind; they had debts at home, too. It was painful. Probably all he needed to avert disaster was some sane advice, a speck of financial insight. I could give him that. I told him to call me before he made any god-awful decisions.

We drank and ate till midnight and went swimming naked while the ladies crawled around looking for shells by the light of the moon. The next morning, we rode with them to the airport, through that beautiful countryside. I was looking at everything, and it was so nice, because we were leaving.

LINDA'S DADDY'S LOADED

M<small>Y WIFE CALLED</small> me at work to say she saw our neighbor in his garden. She was standing in our garden—our house is way up on a hill, you don't realize how high it is until you're up here—and she could see him down there in his fenced-in yard, in shorts and a baseball hat, reading the newspaper. A woman came out of the house in a towel, Linda said, and she took it off and spread it on the ground and started doing exercises on it. Linda said it was weird. The woman wore a bikini, and every once in a while the man looked over at her and said something. He kept lifting one leg, she said, crossing it over the other. The woman sat up and brushed her hair and took off her top, rubbing lotion on her shoulders, and the man got up and lay down next to her and they started making out.

It was hard to see, Linda said, but she could imagine it. I pictured her in the flower bed, with her gloves on and her

gardening shirt and her straw hat and sunglasses and her special knee pads, with the little shovel, and the void look of half recognizing something happening outside her that she wanted or that had somehow grabbed her. And so there she was, sucked in, and she said to herself, What should I do? Should I stop looking? Should I call Mike at work? And then she thought, What if they stay there all day? Then, Linda said, the man rolled off the woman and you could hear them both laughing. She said, "Do you think I should invite them over?"

"Is that why you called me?"

She said, "Why don't we ever do that?"

I didn't know. Linda'd been "retired" for a year. Not working had done this to her. I don't know what you'd call it, but here was the result. I said, "I gotta go." It had been hectic times like you sometimes have at an ad agency, where everybody's going nuts and you rush and rush and the guy you need stays at lunch for three hours. While I was waiting for him to come back I cut off the chewed-up end of my pen cap with a toenail clipper and a piece flew into my eye. It still hurt.

Linda said, "How would you feel if your father was coming to visit us?"

"I don't know." I rubbed my eye. I heard her breathing on the other end. I said, "Is somebody coming to visit us?" She said yes. "Who?"

"My father." She read me a letter that said he'd be at a wedding near us and thought it would be good to come see

our new house. She'd called him back and told him O.K. He'd be here late Saturday. In the letter it said he was bringing "the maid."

She said, "Oh, why is he coming?"

We were living this quiet little life. We had this beautiful house that we built out of her "inheritance." It's not an inheritance—an inheritance is money from a dead person. This was from him. And we didn't "build" the house; we paid somebody else and they built it. It's up there, out of the way of danger, on the edge of a valley of rolling green farms outside Philadelphia. It was everything we'd ever wanted, and we acted happy there. I called her Bunky, she called me Cheese.

"Cheese," she said. "I hate my father."

We had a glorious yard, a beautiful pool, sliding glass doors leading out to a patio, lawn chairs with pillows, a dog, a special electric fence to keep the dog from running away, a thing on his collar to shock him if he tried, track lighting in the kitchen, a marble pastry block. We had a thing to dry the lettuce after you wash it. We had a bug-electrocuting mosquito light. We had a Chevy Tahoe Blazer, and a two-door BMW. We had money, her money. We didn't have to worry about what we bought. We bought the woods behind the house and ran back there with the dog and came home with twigs and leaves stuck to us. We met an interesting group of people when we moved in, all our neighbors who'd built elegant houses out here like ours—the men worked in the city and the women were all psychologists.

We had them over and they had us over, talking and drinking French red wine till two in the morning—it was a fucking blast, discussing famous celebrities roughly our age over roasted chicken, everything great.

The second I met Linda, I knew she was the one. We were so cool together. Everything was easy. She was way better-looking than anyone I'd ever dated before. We'd sit around all night watching TV, making out, eating tacos in our underwear. It was heaven, playing together like children, touching, feeling, learning all the hidden stuff (I hate sports, she smoked PCP in high school). I bought her cheap silly presents every day on my way home from work. She made my balls go slack when she looked at me. Sometimes she looked at me so hard her eyes crossed. It was beautiful. We decided to get married, and then she told me she was rich, and that was terrific. We bought the land and built the house and moved out here.

What were we doing? I gave her this dog, on our first anniversary, and we'd sit on the floor together and talk to it, petting its fur—it was small and soft then. Linda's voice would grow quiet and I'd feel calm, and she'd call it funny names and kiss it; or kiss me, or I'd rub Linda's soft golden forearm and lean over and kiss the back of her silky head, the beautiful smell of shampoo surrounding her, and I could feel the bitterness drain out of me. "Don't think," I'd say to myself. "It's cool." We had an awesome lifestyle. I wanted to enjoy it. The dog was a puppy when we got him,

a furry black ball, but now he was an enormous, shedding mutt; the muscles bulged in a ring around his concrete head as he tore up tennis balls in his jaws and swallowed the pieces. It was my job to walk him at night, and I'd stand in the driveway and watch him piss, and see if he had shit where I had to walk. I'd look at the sky and get lonely. I'd go around shutting off the lights in our big, empty house. That feeling got me every night for at least a second. I'd walk upstairs and hug Linda and hold on, and it took all my troubles away.

FRIDAY AFTER WORK I went to the food store. Linda waxed the floor in the foyer. She vacuumed the carpets, barely able to talk, drained of energy, polishing the table from a lying position on the couch—a scared, pathetic mess. It was awful to watch. I felt sorry for her, and that night we went to bed at nine o'clock. She sat on the covers in a nightshirt with the front unbuttoned and her tits hanging out and put together her Scrabble set and asked me to play. She wanted to organize her brain into letters—"letters that make words"—so her mind could make sense, so she could think, so she could sleep. She said, "I think I'm worried."

"It'll be over before you know it," I said. "Don't think about it."

"Turn up the thermostat," she said. "Turn on the air conditioner. Not the air conditioner. Just the air, just the

fan." She didn't have her contacts in, and she was talking to the wall about two feet to my right, to a dark drape where I'd been standing a few seconds before.

I said, "I'm looking for the switch."

"I like the noise it makes. It calms me, it soothes me, it reminds me of summer and puts me to sleep."

"I'm over here," I said.

"I like the smell."

"All right," I said. "Jesus fucking Christ. Point the light over here so I can see."

I held her and kissed her and told her not to worry—I hated her father, too. I hated my own father more. He was a dickhead. These fathers left a lot to be desired. Linda's face had broken out mysteriously that afternoon, and it was bumpy to the touch, like a rhinoceros. Her breath smelled like hot liverwurst, and while we slept she kept heaving the covers off us onto the floor, her skin was about a million degrees.

SATURDAY MORNING WE were ready. The father wouldn't be here till later, so when there was nothing else to do we got dressed and sat in the living room and stared at each other. Every few minutes the dog walked through. I heard his claws tapping on the kitchen's tile floor, his slobbering sounds, his collar clanging into the food bowl a hundred thousand times.

They pulled into our driveway at four in the afternoon. The sun was still shining. We stood at the open front door.

Her father got out of the car first. He smiled and waited as
the maid came from around the other side to join him. I'd
met him once a long time ago, at a diner in Connecticut;
we'd shaken hands and had coffee, a month before our
wedding, which he wasn't invited to attend. Here again was
Phil's famous face—Phil Shore, the guy from the television-
network evening news—smiling and pointing at his daugh-
ter and me.

Everybody in the family hated him—he was "estranged,"
nobody talked to him anymore. They said he was selfish,
that he'd cheated on his wife for twenty years—there was
crazy stuff the mother accused him of, a secret family he
had hidden in Denmark—but besides that there were real
things, that had been proven. He cut off Linda's sister's col-
lege money—after a screaming fight in which Jeannine
called him "Phil Donahue"—while he went on spending
millions on himself, commuting to work every day in a heli-
copter. And then he dumped the wife. Once every six
months Linda would tell me he'd phoned, and that was it. I
think I talk to my father the same amount, although we
keep it down to that intentionally, to stay on good terms.

Linda's father was wearing gold sunglasses, and he had a
ring of white hair that was fluffed up on the sides. He had
on loafers and linen pants, a white shirt, and a black golf
sweater. He was tan—it was part of his look. The woman
with him had on a long gauzy sundress and sandals, and
as she stepped from behind the car into the sunlight her
body cut a perfect silhouette through the dress. She was

tall and beautiful. She wasn't anybody's maid. She looked like a Dallas Cowboys cheerleader. He'd dumped Linda's mother for this woman. They held hands. She took off her sunglasses and flipped her long brown hair and waved at us. I looked at my wife, whose skin rash was covered up by a dense orange powder. Phil put his hand out and we shook. Linda kissed her father. He introduced the woman—her name was Barbara—and when he spoke his voice was smooth and deep, with a familiar little crackle in it. It dropped and rose, and you found yourself staring at him—just like on television. "Nice to see you, Mike," he said. "The house and yard are lovely." That same careful presentation, the same painstaking delivery.

Linda said to Barbara, "Your hair is a gorgeous color." Barbara said to her, "You have such beautiful blue eyes."

Linda coughed, trying to breathe, and smiled in that rash-makeup, and we went in and showed them the house. Through the bay windows in the living room you looked out on the whole valley; there were grain sheds and farmhouses, and on a road in the distance you could see a truck and a car moving slowly along like toys.

Barbara said, "This is amazing," and put her hand on Linda's father's shoulder and kissed him. She said, "We should do something like this," and he nodded, and Linda and I smiled. The father looked around. He had his hands in his pockets. The lenses of his glasses were fading inside the house.

After the divorce, Phil had given Linda and her sister

each $940,000, and they received a smaller gift from him once a year. It was his success, his fame and money that gave us this house, the land, the cars, the furniture, all our accounts and portfolios and investments—we couldn't have this life on our own; on our own we couldn't have bought the handmade teak porch swing—and he'd never even seen a picture of the place. I wanted to thank him for it—"Thank you for the house, thank you for the cars"—but I didn't.

Barbara told us about the wedding they'd been to, all the fancy dresses, tons of food, and Phil yawned. Linda asked if they even wanted any dinner that night. We said we'd get take-out, and we carried their bags inside and put them in the guest room, and they went in and closed the door.

At six we had drinks on the patio. Barbara and Linda drank wine, and I made vodka tonics for Linda's father and me and put some jazz on the stereo, and the four of us sat down to enjoy the sunset. Phil said something into Linda's ear and went inside, and through the glass patio doors I saw him throw his drink into the kitchen sink. I went in there. He stood at the counter, picking up bottles of booze. He shook one and held it up to the light. I said, "Is your drink O.K.?" He said the vodka was cloudy. "This is it? This stuff is a hundred years old." Linda stood in the doorway with her finger in her mouth. I picked up a bottle of schnapps. He said, "You gotta be kidding me." He blew the dust off a label. Linda went back out and slid the door shut behind

her. There were unopened bottles in the cabinet below, and I saw some other type of vodka and grabbed it. I showed it to him. His eyes were bulging out of his head. His teeth were capped. They looked like Chiclets. He took the bottle out of my hand. He made himself a new drink and cut another piece of lime and went back outside. I followed him. I mixed the next round exactly the way he had; he seemed happy with it, and when I looked over again he was stoned.

It got cool as the sun went down. We put on sweaters. Nobody had anything to say. Barbara smiled at us, bobbing her foot to the music. She asked Linda the name of the man who'd designed the house. Linda yawned with her mouth open. I patted the dog's head. At seven o'clock the delivery guy drove down the driveway with meatball, egg-plant, and sausage and pepper grinders.

Phil followed me out front, and before I could get my wallet out he paid the guy. Then I stood there holding the grinders while he got his briefcase out of the car. He said, "Hey, I like you, Mike. I'm glad to see you with her." I felt a little sweat pop out. It was the most he'd ever said to me. "Thank you," I said. I tried to act somewhat laid-back, I asked him if he still liked to play golf—I couldn't re-member. He said, "She was such a slut in high school." He passed me some folders to carry. "It was obscene," he said, "just the numbers alone," and slammed the car door. Then the dog came loping out of the dark—it loves anyone get-ting in or out of a car—and ran right between his legs. He

raised his briefcase and said, "Get away!" Our dog isn't really trained, and when he smelled the food he came after me, but not before he'd left a big glob of spit on Phil's pants. Phil said, "I don't believe it," and wiped his pants and stomped inside.

We ate, everybody's eyes on the table. Barbara asked Linda, "Do you have any Parmesan?" and Linda exploded out of her chair and over to the kitchen and came back holding the cheese grater in front of her. Phil was quiet. He seemed content to stare at his plate. I asked him about celebrities he'd interviewed; he belched into his fist and sat up, and told us a story about leaving Russia in the sixties with a planeload of journalists—"Just before they locked me in the studio," he said. "Ha-ha"—he was acting slightly more alive. He said they were forced to turn the plane back in midair, and Russian soldiers escorted a guy off who was from one of the Eastern European newspapers and shot him.

I was trying to remember how I knew this story. He said, "That Czech gentleman turned up dead." That was it. This was, word for word, the identical story he told the other time I met him, in that diner. Phil finished his beer, hunched over in his chair. He didn't look the way he looked on TV. He looked old. I'm sure he was tired. His eyes were all red. But there were other, subtle differences. I watched him swallow. Up close, he was mostly ears and sagging eyelids.

I nodded along to the end of the story. He said, "When

we got home from that one, we got out the vodka and drank." Déjà vu that line, too. I stood up and got the vodka bottle from the kitchen and slammed it down in front of him. Everybody laughed. I wondered if he'd ever been on that plane in the first place. I pictured him lying on the couch in his office, masturbating to an image of himself dressed in a Russian Army uniform, himself dressed as the airplane pilot, himself getting shot as the Czech guy. I thought how boring it must've been for his daughters to grow up listening to this egomaniac tell the same dull stories every night—even though he didn't, because he was never around. Across from me, Linda didn't seem to mind. She had a dim, unconscious half smile on her lips. He pulled at the sandwich and dabbed his chin with his napkin, chewing slowly. We finished, finally—yahoo!—and Linda asked who wanted coffee, and he wiped his mouth with the napkin and folded it and dropped it on the floor, and said he was tired and told everybody good night and went to the guest room.

In bed that night I kissed Linda on her head. I said, "It's going O.K., I think." She was lying on her side, not facing me. There was all this tension between us. "You're doing great," I said. She nodded. I said, "I'm proud of you."

"Uh-huh."

"Your dad's terrific."

"He's a one-trick pony," she said.

"I love you."

She looked at me. "What a charmboat," she said, and turned back and went to sleep.

With no rash on her face, she's beautiful. Her face is the kind women would kill for, what plastic surgeons try to emulate. No kidding. And I'm not bragging: I think she's damaged because of it. She can be a pain in the ass. She doesn't know who to trust, so she has to trust me, but if you took an X ray of the inside of her soul you'd see loose pieces, with unmatched edges, floating around inside her. Beautiful women are a pain in the ass. In some ways, they're worse off than ugly women—even ugly men, even ladies with full beards—because under their laser scrutiny everybody is horrible and gross.

Linda's skin is powdery warm brown silk. Picture gold. Her chin is pointed. Her cheekbones are sloped. She has blue eyes like a plastic doll's—circular, sparkling clear-glass marbles—and long eyelashes, a wide mouth, soft lips, and long thick brown hair. She has a battery of predictable human expressions. She's talked about becoming a school-teacher, or a psychologist, like the neighbors on either side of us, women who do something, who found a skill. I wish she'd do that. I wish she would. She took time off from her old job—she hated clothing sales, driving to malls, selling Donna Karan—and then talked herself into retiring for-ever, but she can't stay retired forever.

You know that pain you feel when you see an incredibly beautiful face: You look at her and you want to know what

she's thinking and you're sitting there guessing and you don't even come close? You have to kiss her and hold her sweet face in your hands and shove her down somewhere and get on top of her and make her all yours—even when she *is* yours? Even when she loves you, too? Even when she's your wife and she gave you everything she had? I look at her and I feel that pain. If I had it to do again, I'd marry a woman who didn't have such remarkable luck, who was born with a face like a horse, a face like a Russian carrot farmer, with whiskers, who maybe blossomed later in life, someone who was forced to be a human being before giving up, or a fat one, even, so she doesn't snap at you.

SUNDAY MORNING I drove in to work with the excuse of grabbing a disk and spent the day there, editing videotape on the computer. When I came home, the cars were sitting in the driveway exactly where I'd left them. I found Linda kneeling in the garden, with Barbara lying on a chaise in the sun nearby, looking into the sky with my binoculars. I asked where the father was. They said he was in the guest room on the phone. I went over to Linda and gave her a kiss. It made a hollow, sucking noise. She looked at me, panicked.

I said, "Relax."

She said, "I know."

Her skin looked worse. It was shiny from ointment. She stared ahead, her neck veins bulging. "He ate all the ice today," she said.

I said, "That's O.K."

She said, "He chomps it," and moved her jaws up and down, showing me. She was looking to me for some kind of recognition.

I said, "The refrigerator makes more automatically."

Linda sighed, panting. She said, "I feel like I'm five years old again."

I said, "You're O.K. It's fine."

She said, "I want to run away," and I said, "Not without me you're not," and she said, "We can't go anywhere. We live here."

I said, "I know."

She went inside to get dinner ready. Barbara followed her.

I put on my trunks, went outside, and swam back and forth in the pool until I could feel the pressure of my goggles forcing my eyeballs out of their sockets. I got out and sat in a chair for a few minutes, leaning hard into the backrest, trying to get the plastic tubes of the chair to explode. Then I just looked out, unwinding, glad to be home. I watched the air above the valley, following a bird as it glided around catching pockets of air down there, as it made itself rigid and floated. I wanted to see these people get in their car and leave. I listened to the two women's high voices through the window in the kitchen and tried to make out what they were saying. I stood up and popped the pool water out of my ear and went inside.

The father was still not out of his room. It appeared that

nothing had happened here today among this group, except worse hives. Phil and Barbara were leaving first thing Tuesday—he had to interview King Hussein in a hospital in New Jersey, and I guess this was their layover. I wondered if Phil had some other reason for the visit. What was it? Why backtrack lost causes? Why do it half-assed? Let it go. Send an e-mail.

Linda stood over the stove, with that rash-face. She was trying not to freak, and currently this stage was holding. I would've liked to be in Bermuda, with a hash pipe surgically attached to my lips, but I was trying, too. Even the dog was trying, smiling at everybody and wagging his tail, not shitting his monuments in the driveway for me to hurdle. We were trying to be an upbeat household. Linda painted the chicken parts, humming loudly. Barbara chopped the salad. She asked if I was hungry. I said I was starving.

The father came out, and we mixed drinks and carried them into the living room and turned on the news. He wore the same black sweater, with a clean, pressed teal-blue golf shirt underneath. He praised the TV anchorman, his weekend sub. "A black guy like him can take it as far as he wants," he said, and stared at the screen and kept his leg jiggling, even during commercials. I got us some peanuts and watched him watch the news. He yelled, "The Hague," when the anchor called it "The Hog," and he laughed and slapped the couch. "Pronunciation, mon frair!" he said, and

switched off the show, relaxed and happy, when it ended a minute later. He asked me again exactly what I did for a living, and I told him that my agency did advertising and video production—no big deal, although we'd gotten a new client recently and the account was bigger than everything else combined.

He said, "That's exciting."

I said, "*Ucchh.* They want to shake everything up." He smiled. I said, "I hate that."

The client made some computer crap, I told him—I had no idea what. I just produced cable-TV commercials on video, cheap stuff. The other guys handled the business.

He put a big handful of peanuts into his mouth and leaned very close to me and chewed and breathed his bitter old peanut-and-vodka, coffee-stained breath in my face. "It's tremendous," he said. "The structure of business is changing forever."

I said, "Oh, yeah?"

He said, "Universal access to information on the Internet—that blows my mind." He tapped the side of his head. I stared at his Chiclets. He started talking about where my agency should bid for new business, like the defense industry.

I said, "Yeah, excellent, wow."

He said, "You gotta be aggressive."

I said, "That's right." He seemed psyched as hell. He grabbed the back of my neck and yanked it.

"I really like you, Mike," he said. He turned around and yelled to the women in the kitchen, "How's it going in there!" They both went, "Fine."

Linda once told me how he could go for days without sleep, how he napped on the floor of his office, how he screamed at his reporting staff so hard one time that he broke a blood vessel in his face and fainted and had to be carried out of the meeting by paramedics. But his news program had revolutionized the way networks reported information to us. He invented the informal patter that anchors you see today are using—he started that, he battled for it, he believed in it, and he won. He loved his job.

I asked if I could show him some videos I'd made, and handed him an award plaque I'd won a few years ago. He held it and looked at it. We watched some tape of a commercial for a computer distributor; I told him I'd wanted it to look like documentary footage.

He asked if I was interested in the media. I said yes. He said, "I could set something up."

I said, "Like what?"

"I'll call our Philly station," he said. "You'd probably start small—assembling footage from the network feed, that sort of thing," and I said, "Wow." The women called and said dinner was ready, and he put the award down on the couch.

At dinner there were candles on the table, baked chicken in orange sauce and raisins, vegetables with ginger and toasted black seeds on them, rice pilaf, a dense-

looking, flat chocolate cake for dessert. Linda opened a bottle of wine. I raised my glass and said, "A toast." Everybody looked at me. I didn't mean I would *make* a toast. The bread Linda had just baked was steaming under the light. I started giggling in my high-pitched voice. She opened her mouth tightly and blanched. I was trying to think. Linda said, "What's a good toast?"

"To these two wonderful young people," Phil said. Barbara said "Hear! Hear!" and we clinked glasses and started passing around the food. Linda watched her father pick up his fork. He took a bite and said everything was champ.

Barbara said, "When are you going to have kids?" Linda froze—we weren't ready for any kids—but before she could really freak, Phil started telling us about the night Linda was born. "I had one foot out the door to Hanoi," he said. "But your mother . . ." He waved his hand at his lap to mean her stomach, the baby, something below the equator. "You almost came out in the driveway, you dope," he said.

Linda was blushing, watching him, wide-eyed. He said he was glad to see his firstborn, alive and healthy. He picked up his wineglass and said, "My secretary just had a baby. It's too small. You were a big, fat, beautiful baby, and you were always staring at me with your gorgeous eyes." He lifted Linda's hand and kissed it.

Linda started to cry. She got up and went to the bathroom and came back a minute later with the rice pot and another bottle of wine. Phil cut off the foil and opened it, and told us how he got beaten up by black kids when he

was growing up poor in the Bronx in the thirties. "You ever been hit in the head with a baseball bat?" he asked me. I tried to think of something: When I was eleven, I fell down the stairs. "I guess not," I said. He told us about fighting in Korea; he mentioned his first night on national news, in 1962; he told us how he hung out with Cronkite; he described Bobby Kennedy's funeral procession down Fifth Avenue. He said hookers used to come through the newsroom to see the network bigshots; a lot of these guys were ruined by money, he said.

He poured more wine. "Linda," he said, "I discussed a deal with my lawyers." He paused. I didn't know what would come next; I pictured him throwing us out of this house, taking everything, boarding it up. "I made an investment that worked out the way I hoped it would, and I'm transferring the funds to you and Jeannine." We both said thanks. "It's done," he said. "It's a nice sum." Linda said, "Thank you, Daddy." He said, "Close to eight hundred thousand dollars apiece." I felt a wild pain shoot into my rectum, and I picked up my glass, staring at it as if there was some incredible thing dancing around in the wine. Linda said, "God, that's a lot of money." Her expression didn't change.

"I've spoken to your mother a number of times," he said. "I've seen her twice this year." He said he liked the way she had redecorated the old house. "We've made up," he said. "We're O.K. now. I don't know whether that matters to you or not." Linda shrugged her shoulders and

smiled, and wiped her eyes with her napkin. "It's not the end of the world," he said.

"No," Linda said. Her voice broke.

It was midnight before we got up. We'd drunk four bottles of wine. Linda went and hugged her father, and he took her by the arm and led her outside to the patio. Barbara and I cleared off the table. She said, "He's a wonderful, wonderful man."

I said, "Yeah."

She said, "He treats me as good as he treats them." We were drunk as hell. We kept banging into each other. Outside, I saw Linda nodding to Phil as he spoke—it seemed like a huge relief. We ran hot water on the big pots and left them, and everybody went to bed.

Lying there, I could feel Linda's warm skin through her nightgown as she hugged me. My stomach was full from all that dinner and drinking, and I was tired and shitfaced and falling asleep, and I shoved her to the other side of the bed. When I opened my eyes again my wife was staring at me, shaking her head, smiling. I said, "You O.K.?" She nodded. She looked demented. I said, "I have to go to work in the morning." She got up—it made the bed bounce—and started brushing her hair out.

She said, "I love my daddy." She came over and sat on my leg, and pulled out matches and lit a candle. She kept moving and waking me up. She was like a big, hot cat next to me. She said, "I'm happy, Cheese."

When I woke up again, Linda was repeating my name,

tapping on the skin of my upper lip with her index finger. I jumped. She said she wanted to go for a walk in the woods in the middle of the night. I blew out the candle. I told her to be quiet or I'd kill her; it was late, and tomorrow was going to be a heavy day at work. "Please, Bunky!" I said, but she begged me, so I got up and pulled the quilt off our bed and we stepped outside through the sliding glass doors and lay in the grass under our bedroom window. She pulled up my T-shirt and licked my stomach, and put her head down my pants and sucked on my completely flat penis for a while, until she gave up and laid her head on my gut. The mosquitoes were hovering over us, not touching our skin. It was cool out there. I held her face. We fell asleep and woke up later with dew on us. We crawled back inside, and I moved the alarm ahead from six to seven.

WHEN I GOT to work Monday, there was a message from Millhouse saying I should go to his office. He waved me in, sitting on the edge of his desk. Chip, our account supervisor, and Laura, the personnel manager, came in. Dean—Millhouse's partner and our lawyer—followed them with folders and sat on the couch.

Millhouse said, "The video department's a loser for the second year in a row. We're dumping it." Everybody was quiet.

"Oh, God," I said.

He said, "The structure of business is changing anyway." They were watching me. Chip jumped in and explained

that, instead, I'd be overseeing "virtual-media services." He wanted me to write a brochure. I should talk about our mission, he said, and he thought I should mention technology and computers. He said, "Make it sales-y."

I said, "Do what?"

Chip said, "I need it by Thursday." He looked at Millhouse and back at me. "Don't worry. You'll figure it out."

I said, "I'm a filmmaker."

Chip blinked. He said, "Can you do a website?"

I said, "Whatever," and walked out.

I went down the hall to my office. I shut the door, and five minutes later I walked back down the hall and leaned into Millhouse's doorway and said, "Are you gonna farm out video to somebody else?" He shrugged. He was on the phone. I said, "Am I that bad?" He covered up the mouthpiece and said, "Are you blind? I'm talking!" He's terrible with people. I packed my briefcase with papers and told Donna at the switchboard that I was sick and ran down to the garage and got my car.

I drove through the city. It was almost lunchtime. The lab was supposed to return film for two spots this afternoon so we could synch the sound, quarterly expense reports for my department were due at five o'clock, and we were having a barbecue that night with Linda's father and Barbara and six of our closest neighbors. I hadn't seen these people in weeks; I wanted everything to be cool. The scene at home was tricky enough. I was wearing a beautiful darkgreen cashmere turtleneck sweater Linda had bought me,

and the sweat was pouring out of my armpits, rolling down my sides. I had the air conditioner on full blast, sweating my ass off. I kept calling my voice mail at work and hanging up. I called home. Phil, of all people, answered.

"Can I talk to Linda?"

He said, "I'm on the phone."

I said, "Guess what? Is your offer still good from last night?"

Phil said, "I don't follow you. Look, I'm on another call. Just call back."

I drove around, staring at my car's reflection in passing store windows. I was an idiot for bringing up that stuff with Linda's father. I thought of everything he'd done—broadcasting live from wars, hosting presidential debates, kneeling at the coffins of kings in photos on the covers of every newspaper in the world. Every time I saw a guy in a car on his cellular phone, I flipped out. I needed something immediately—a hug from my wife—and I jetted home.

THEY WEREN'T THERE. I remembered they'd gone to pick up steaks for the barbecue that night, and I sat down to wait.

The dog came over and stood in front of me. He needed to be brushed. He had a cow's head and a long coat—he looked like a dusty, exploded buffalo rug. I said, "Come here, Ripley." He stared at me with his black eyes, and I thought of how brain-dead he was and yet, even so, was

able to engender love in every living thing around him. I hugged him and patted his head.

I let him out the patio door and went outside, across the lawn, and lay down in a quiet spot back in the woods. Ripley came around the long way and took a piss in the pine needles two feet from my head. I jumped up and yelled, "Get out of here!" and kicked him in the ass, and he ran over behind a bush and stared at me. We were never mean to our dog, and he didn't know what I meant by it. But I didn't mean anything by it. I just kicked him.

We used to be a team, Linda and me. We shared an apartment for eight hundred bucks a month. She worked. She cooked spaghetti. No weekly food-delivery service, no personal trainer, no aromatherapy, no bond portfolio, no unborn-student college fund, no self-published recipe book, no invisible hair replacement, no eight thousand magazines flung at our door every month. I'd never been happy on the dole. I went over to the dog. He started to tiptoe away, and I grabbed him by the collar. "Stay, you fucker!" I said. He dropped to the ground in a submissive posture, and I leaned over and put my knee behind his head. His tongue went out, and he hacked and choked and kept trying to back up. I put my hand through his collar and twisted it, cutting off everything. He yelped. "Go ahead, you crybaby," I said. He tried to lick my hand. I heard a door slam—they were back. With one final shove, I pushed myself off him and tried to break his neck, both. The dog

jumped up, hacking and spitting, and took off into the woods.

When I got to the house, it was obvious that something was wrong: Barbara wouldn't talk to anyone, and Phil wouldn't look at her. Linda went past me into the kitchen with some bags. She didn't ask why, on a Monday at noon, I was home. I said, "What's going on?"

She said, "It started at breakfast." Phil had on a U.S. Navy baseball hat that said USS NIMITZ CVN-68 stitched in gold. He circled the island counter in the kitchen and pushed the thing on the refrigerator door to fill his glass with ice cubes. He looked over into the living room at the back of Barbara's head and said, "Keep pouting, Princess. Go right ahead." She didn't move. "You're making a spectacle," he said. Barbara got up and picked up her sunglasses and closed the guest-room door behind her.

Linda looked at me. Her eyes were yellow. She said, "I can't cope anymore."

I said, "Oh, really? That's fucking unbelievable," and stared right back at her. I wanted to smack her face.

Phil went over and picked up the remote and turned on the TV. He stood there behind the couch staring at it. Linda walked past me. She said, "Daddy, turn that off."

She took the remote out of his hand. She said, "Christ." She stood there, staring at him. He removed his hat and rested it on his chest. His freckled bald head looked flat and smooth. He said, "What."

"Go talk to her," Linda said. "Now." She put the remote down on the back of the couch and pointed her finger over at the guest-bedroom door, sort of crookedly, with a bent finger, like an old witch's; her hand shook. "Go," she said, and continued the incantation, "because this is pathetic. You're not doing this here. You be nice."

He wet his lips and looked at her. Linda placed her hands on her hips. He said, "Yeah, yeah." He put the hat on again and slid it back and went over to the guest-bedroom door. He knocked and said, "Barbara," and went in.

Linda came over and stood in front of me. She was grinning like crazy. She said, "Did I do good?"

I said, "Yep."

"I took charge of my life."

I said, "Yeah."

She said, "What's wrong?" Her rash was glowing.

I said, "What do you think would happen if the world stopped letting you pant in their face?" She stopped smiling. I went outside to find the dog, to make up for choking him.

THE BARBECUE THAT night was a mellow affair. The neighbors all came and everybody was cool. They were thrilled and giddy to meet Linda's famous dad, and there was a ring of people around him all night, joking, laughing, asking his advice. Linda cooked steak and spun around in her new dress, grabbing her dad and showing him off,

introducing her friends by their professions and showing them off, too. She'd picked up some steroids from the doctor, and her skin was better. We stayed away from each other. There was that jolly group, like, over there, and I was over here, talking to Barbara about her exercise routine. She played with the dog, who was rolling on his back, drooling, with this beautiful woman scratching his pink belly.

Phil had made the call to the affiliate. The deal was done. I said thanks. "You ready to rumble?" he said. I said yes. "You happy?" he said. I said yes. Absolutely.

I think of that mean thing I said to Linda—what was that all about? It's like there's a bird in my mouth, screeching. Maybe one day I'd open my mouth and it would come out like a flying hockey puck. I don't know, some nights I'd like to shoot out all the lights of this fucking house.

But hey, there's plenty of time for that. She's still there, my cute wife, whom I love: humming and singing to herself when there is tension in the house; or laughing, when all the doors are open, talking to her sister on the phone in the living room while I finish my dinner. We're going to be happy more than not, Linda and me. We're going to get this thing right. Even when it backfires, you don't necessarily hate someone for very long.

THERE SHOULD BE A
NAME FOR IT

LYNN'S ROASTING A chicken. She takes out garlic, chili powder, and a lime. "What's that for?" I say. "There are pine nuts above your head," she says. I hand them down to her. Now she butters the pan. She's got the coriander in a bag, cloves, curry, and two oranges. Then other green herbs. Jesus Christ, I'm thinking, all that crap for the chicken.

"All that's for the chicken?"

"What?"

"What? That." I'm pulling on my eyebrow hair. It's a nervous habit, but I feel like plucking these long curly ones. "All that goes on the chicken?"

She rinses off her hands and says, "This is a recipe from my mom."

It's early summer. It's afternoon, and the kitchen is the brightest room in this house. It's like a greenhouse in here,

very sunny. The house itself is small and cheap, though a hundred and fifty years ago somebody planted a sycamore on the front lawn. Protected from the wind and fed by sun and water, the plant grew into a giant. The limbs stretch up—it's like an elephant, white tusks against the sky.

"Up we go," she says, upending the chicken. She pulls a wax-paper bag from inside it like an envelope and drops it in the sink.

"What the hell is that?" I say. Lynn wipes her forehead with her wrist. She takes the bag out of the sink and tears it open, spilling the contents into her hand. It's meat—it looks like tongues.

"Oh, my God."

"It's chicken livers. See?"

She flicks them with her finger. It's three glistening pieces of purple meat, but not at all like steak. They look like they were alive five minutes ago. She holds one. She seems to enjoy touching it.

"O.K., get rid of it." Lynn puts the bag and the livers in the garbage. She says, "You make it with onions. My mother loves it."

"Yeah."

This is the whole chicken, an entire animal. Like, I haven't exactly seen this done before by a person my age. We're both kids. We don't know how to cook this stuff. In all the time we've been living together, Lynn's never cooked a whole chicken.

I'm leaning close enough to her that I can smell her

shampoo. Her hair is thick and reddish brown, full and shiny, and her skin is the color of creamy tan suede. Mexican mother, Irish father. You know how they airbrush the skin of ladies in *Playboy*? I see Lynn's body every day, I look at her skin up close, I've had my eye an inch above her stomach or her shoulder or her calf, and it's flawless. It's golden skin. Every morning after her shower, Lynn comes and stands in front of me—I'm either getting dressed or making notes for work—then she turns around and I rub cream across her shoulders, underneath the bra straps, bright-white fabric against her tan skin.

She cuts the fat off the chicken, that makes sense, but with scissors, of all things. She holds it like a little playmate, flipping it over, rocking it under the faucet. She washes out the hole in it, pouring some little pieces of red guts into the sink, shaking out the dried blood or cartilage that runs down and sticks in the drain. Sickening. Then she tears off a piece of brown paper bag and folds it, dabbing the outside of the chicken.

"What are you doing?" I ask.

"It gets the old oil out of the skin."

"Old oil? What, like sweat?"

"No, not like sweat," she says. "Like sweat? Chickens don't sweat."

"I know."

"I'm cooking you dinner and you're gonna stand here and give me shit?"

"No! No way. This is gonna be sensational."

I love her. Man! I really do. She's a pistol. It's not placating love, it's really passionate love. Uncharted territory, yes, definitely. But that's what love is—undefined.

"Move aside, termite," she says to me, grabbing the bottle of olive oil.

"Termite," I say. "Good one."

I love how she says that— "Are you gonna give me shit?" That's funny. The answer is yes, I am.

Lynn's awesome, though. She knows what she's thinking, and she knows what you're thinking. She's got you. She's a keeper, as they say. I want to keep her.

"Or would you rather I'd left the feathers on?"

I say, "You're the chef." I mean, whatever this girl touches turns to gold.

Say something bad happened to her, and we have no control over it. All of a sudden there's a situation. Hang on, let me start this over.

It's hard to explain—poor kid—a month ago Lynn had to get an abortion. What a lead balloon. What a joke. It ain't no joke.

"Give me that," she says, pointing at the pepper, and I hand it to her. She rubs chili powder on the skin. Now the paprika, now salt, now some other stuff.

In Spanish, the word is *aborto*, a foreign word that even I can master and pretty easy for Celia, Lynn's mother, to yell at her a few times over the phone. *"Aborto! Aborto! Clak-ata-clak-ata-clak-ata."*

Lynn called home. It was night, we were lying in bed,

and I heard everything from my side. I wanted to help, but what could I do? You don't interfere with a family. Lynn nodded into the phone, picked up a pencil and stared at it.

"Mom. We already decided."

"Goddamn it!" I heard Celia say. "You slut. You and your jackass boyfriend."

After two minutes, Lynn hung up. She didn't say anything.

"Jackass boyfriend?" I said.

"She said to tell you she hates you."

"Thanks."

In my mind, I saw Celia stomping barefoot through her newly carpeted house with the antenna phone and her 1950s bouffant hairdo and ten pounds of eye shadow, shaking her fist, saying, "Goddamn jackass," meaning me, blaming it on me.

LYNN AND I have a normal sex life. Whatever that means. Sex is never normal with anyone, it's bizarre, it's wiggly meats, but Lynn was a virgin when we met. And then a couple of months went by, and we were invited to her parents' for Christmas.

We drove from Colorado to Ohio. It's twenty-two hours by car. You know how it is when you go on a road trip—you're going to a new place together. After five or six hours, the inside of the car smelled like BO; my ass began to hurt; my legs felt like concrete; there were sunflower seeds all over the floor. More miles, and soon we were spit-

ting the shells on each other. Two o'clock in the morning, shit-bag road stop, I'm buying cigarettes in Michigan. Lynn's standing next to me in a pink pajama top and jeans, sunflower-seed shells in her hair, which is all sticking up in knots in the back from her sleeping on it. She gave me two candy fireballs; her hand was warm and clammy. Outside, no cars passed by. It was silent. It wasn't particularly cold for December. There was the gas station and then nothing for miles.

We stood in the unfamiliar light of the store in the middle of nowhere, lost. It was at about that time that I felt anything could happen. Me and my girlfriend, Lynn, on our first road trip together. When you're twenty-three, a road trip is the highlight of your life. I held on to her hand. It's the same person, and she's great, but she seemed different all of a sudden, three-dimensional. Like a person you've just met for the first time and would like to get to know. As we drove off, the car went over a speed bump and out of the corner of my eye I saw Lynn's boobs shake.

They put me in the guest room in the basement. The room had white wicker furniture and green-and-silver jungle wallpaper. Mold in the squishy rug. We'd packed our clothes into the same suitcase, and as I dug through it for my contact-lens holder I came across a bunch of Lynn's underwear. I took a pair out and held them up to the light, weightless flowered cotton panties. They had a lacy edge. They were clean and cute and smelled like powder. Eleven o'clock at night I'm sitting on the bed in the dank base-

ment, white wicker furniture and green jungle wallpaper, the underwear crumpled against my nose and mouth, tracing swirl patterns in the stucco ceiling. I really loved her. Two floors above me my girlfriend lay sleeping, down the hall from her mother and father. I never put pressure on Lynn, for I knew that would be wrong, and yet she must've felt safe. We'd begun to build up trust. This is the part where Lynn loses her virginity. It was the holiday season. The stage was set.

Lunchtime, Celia had made a Mexican specialty, a casserole, a savory thing, cheap cuts of fatty meat, bone chips, dog lips, and I went into the bathroom to get a stain off my pants. Lynn came in to help me, and we both ended up naked from the waist down. She got up on the sink, both of us a little self-conscious, trying to be quiet, except I was so excited my feet itched, the thing so hard it felt like it was pulling off me of its own power. Lynn's like kicking my jeans, she was like Don't come inside me, she was like drooling, her eyes rolled back into her head, kind of grunting, her legs around my waist. And there were her parents—Celia and Phil sitting outside the door sopping up the orange grease on their plates from their Mexican lasagna. Man, it was something. Lynn said, "I'm supposed to be a virgin, you bastard. My mother is in the next room. Stop it right now. Stop it before I faint," laughing. "Somebody, help." I almost fainted myself, both of us leering and hot as monkeys.

It's terrible the way kids work off their parents.

That week was the best sex I ever had in my life: Celia knocking on the door to Lynn's room during afternoon-nap time, me beneath the blanket, Lynn saying, "I'll be right out, Mom, I'm getting dressed," Celia saying, "Where's Jack, honey?" *and really not knowing where I was!* See? That's why I love the Midwest. Such a dreamy lack of a clue. That's what happens in the Ohio River valley, even to a transplanted Mexican with citizenship. I'm from New York, where dead people are not that dumb. These folks are idiots. I mean innocent. Other friends of their family would come by, I'd run down to the basement to bring up extra chairs, and I'd feel it dribbling in my pants. Once the first one was out of the way, we did it every time Phil and Celia turned their backs. Every time they went to the food store. They had to go back to the food store so many times because we were eating everything in the refrigerator and losing weight at the same time. Their whole house must still smell from our spooge. I picture that dumpy suburban street—the snow melting in rivers of mud everywhere, her dad walking around in that fisherman hat, the smell of new wall-to-wall carpet everywhere in their house—and I get an exciting feeling inside. It's like the first time we did it all over again.

LYNN HOLDS THE chicken's weight in one hand and rubs a stick of butter around it with the other, like a deodorant stick, almost. She sprinkles it with lime, rubbing gently with her other hand around its back and rump. It makes

me squeamish sitting there, like it might get up all of a sudden and tap my shoulder, but Lynn's got a pretty sure grip on it. She grabs it by the cavity, sticks it on its back in the pan, and throws in a bunch of herb leaves and pine nuts. Then she cuts up an onion and an orange with the skin still on.

My office mate Amy told me, after she had her baby, how similar an uncooked chicken felt in her hands to the body of her daughter. She said how she held it, rubbing olive oil on it, under the wings, around the thighs, with soft loose pink skin, the small, protective rib cage. It was the same weight and size as her baby. She said even the elbows had a similar feel in her wet hands. She said it was too funny, so she loaded her camera, naked Elizabeth lying next to the chicken on Amy's leather coat, and all the groceries piled up around them. She stood on a chair and got the two birds on film.

Lynn is standing at the sink now, measuring out rice, and looking at me with those bright-green eyes that say, "I know what I'm doing here." She looks like an angel. My knees begin to buckle, and I just want to put her down on the kitchen floor and start the trouble all over again. I want to bare her breast and nod on her nipple. I'm her baby. She's my baby. Everybody's somebody's baby. Let's make a baby.

Lynn says, "What else besides rice?"

"Do you want salad?" I say.

In April we put a garden in the backyard. The land be-

hind our house is flat. It gets both sun and shade. The grass is long and lush and light green, and right now there are some dandelions. It'll need mowing soon. The garden was our team project, although the day we rented the tiller Lynn was sick and I did everything, and I'd just as soon have Fritos over a vegetable any day of the week. But we both like looking at the garden.

After dinner we go and check out the garden, walking between the rows, careful of where we step. Sometimes she'll pull weeds. When it gets dark we lie on the cold metal basement doors and watch the sky. Above us, the clouds are silently on the move, backlit by the moon. The smell of cut grass is everywhere. The sweet smell and the crickets, and the slick noise of lawn sprinklers hissing in the dark. Grass smells good. There should be a name for it.

"I'll get the salad," I say. There's a basket we use for the vegetables. I take it off the top of the refrigerator.

"I'll do it," Lynn says. "I'm in the mood." She pulls the basket out of my hands and goes out the back door, the glass doorknob banging against the wall.

The sun is going down. Flat, ginger-colored light is sprayed against every surface inside the kitchen, across the counters and the refrigerator door and the walls that are the color of yellow wine. I hear her say hello to Whiskey, the cat. The people next door own him. Strange name for a cat.

It's Tuesday. It's almost seven. Time to eat.

We said we'd get a cat, but what I really want is a dog—

dogs are better—but cats are less permanent. If we had to move, you could give the cat away, or leave it. No one would do that to a dog, and anyway it's against the law. A dog would starve to death.

Our difficulties began one night three months ago. I know the exact night. Lynn came home from class and said, "I just got my period. It's so early this month." She said something cute like "You don't have to worry about rubbers for a while." I do worry about rubbers. They are my downfall. We did it that night, no rubber. There was an instant—I remember it—when I was deciding whether or not to actually go for it. I followed a certain line of reasoning, and remembered what she said, twinkled over the risks, and then blew my nuts out. It was something to behold. I really enjoyed myself, oink oink, drowning in it. But then her period disappeared the next day. Or I should say it never came.

She was ovulating.

Let me lay this out again. She ovulated that night, thus the dot of blood. Then we did it. Bingo. You morons, you fucking biologists.

She was pregnant. It was April. I'd just turned twenty-four. I'd never been near an abortion clinic. And Colorado's not the laid-back, liberal-Jew neck of the woods I come from. This here's the American West. I work for a software designer, but I've seen guys in spurs all duded up like *Deliverance* on a Friday night.

I felt desperate and called my parents. My mom told me

how in Florida a pro-life group stood outside a women's clinic with a bullhorn, yelling, "If you come out now we'll shoot you, but your unborn child will be spared!" Congress had just blocked the abortion pill for the eighty-second time. She told me that what we were doing was O.K. Her voice made me homesick.

The thing about New York City is everything's so jam-packed. It's the crowds, there are so many bums, dead people practically lying on the street. In the winter you die from the cold wind, in the summer you die from the heat. The breeze stinks, the people smell like piss, there's the traffic. It's impossible to park. Everybody's in a rotten mood. No place to hide.

In Colorado, the sun always shines. The sky is usually blue, and when we hang our clean clothes on the line in the backyard they dry in an hour. When you smell them they're crisp and smell like air. The mountains are to the west of town. This is a new town, 120 years old. They shot indigenous peoples to settle this town. You drive up into the Rockies and see powdery snow on the side of the road. Toward the eastern part of Colorado there are cornfields that go clear across the Midwest, I think. That yonder there is Kansas, I reckon. Anyway, it's flat, and kind of stunning from inside a car, cows and fields and vistas slashing out in every direction, and the sky above you is a flawless ceiling. God, you think, this would be perfect, if only . . . if only I had more money, if only it were a couple of years from now, if only Lynn and I were married, or were ready to get mar-

ried, if I had more friends here—but old friends—or decent places to hang out at, or more of a feeling of what's next.

They wouldn't let us come in to the clinic yet. She wasn't far enough along. We had to wait almost two weeks to have it done. Seven and a half weeks is the magic number, for all you peckerheads taking notes. Anything less, it's a speck of unremovable dust. Lynn ate saltines before she got out of bed every day, and I brought her a cold glass of club soda. Our friend Tina taught her that.

I'd walk in, hand her the saltines, and sit and look at this girl I've been sleeping next to for months and months—five months by then—and I hated her. She was sick now, and I was sick of her, I hated her little puffy knocked-up ass, she looked like a worried old hag, and out of nowhere I'm just not so sure of anything. Why I all of a sudden don't love her. Because there's something about her that I'm definitely not too sure about. What if she turns into her mother? Celia's a joke.

They say a pregnant woman looks radiant. Lynn went around for two weeks, agitated and angry and with an upset stomach, but she really did look radiant—it was like a cosmetics expert had done something to her face. Her cheeks were flushed all day, and her eyes were as bright as green candy. I can't explain the difference. I kept catching myself staring. For those two weeks she was nauseous and pissed off. Added to that, I was still in training for my job, we were not married or engaged or anything, and Lynn really

didn't know, ha-ha, was she maybe ready to be a mother? Maybe she wasn't and maybe she was. Is twenty-two too young? She toyed with the idea while lolling around in the bath, conditioning her hair. Well, I knew. I'm sure. Please ask me.

Out the window now the sun is setting. It's the summer of 1995. I see Lynn is crouched between the vegetables, picking peas and pulling up weeds.

This garden is a pretty thought—it's the nicest thing I've ever done. We have snap peas growing along one row. I read in the paper that they like to climb, so I built a trellis beside the row, crisscross lattice-wood slats, about two feet tall. I painted it white. We have eggplants, squash, tomatoes, and yellow flowers, and next year we'll plant tubers. When I hate Lynn, or when I can't stand to look at her or be near her, when I feel putrid, when I wish God would just erase me, I look at the garden. When she gets angry or yells about something terrible I did and we're fighting, I look out the window at that thing we made, the garden, at the lawn when it's been mowed and raked and looks like a putting green, cool and flat and smells sweet. You want to lie down on it and tear the grass up with your hands. Sometimes I think I'm just about ready to kill her.

How come I never do what I'm supposed to do? How come everything I do is such a fucking disaster? Doesn't anybody get what they want? And that line of hers about how she might want to have it. She came out of the bath-

tub with a towel on her head, fluffing her hair. "Honey," she said. She never called me "Honey" before in her life. "Honey, I've been thinking about our child." I could feel all the blood draining from my head. White flecks on the edges of my vision. There was a narrow window of opportunity there, before I calmed myself, where different pictures whizzed into my mind. Blood, knives, handcuffs, that sort of thing. I told her, You have it alone, honey darling, in your own purple dream world—I'll be in Australia by the time the thing comes out.

There's the immense Colorado sky, there's the grass, there's the clothes on the line, fruit hanging ripe in the trees, the smell of wet cut grass. The land ripping out flat to the Mississippi with the sun leering on top in every direction. And you're standing above it, a million miles from bumper-to-bumper commuter-nightmare New York. You're not there anymore, though, you're here, at the foot of the Rockies, cow-town college town on the American prairie. Great American steer farm. Steroid-fat cows. Transistor radios in barns, cows chewing all night long.

There were five of us in the room during the procedure: the doctor, her assistant, the hand-holder, me, and, of course, Lynn. She was the star. This was her show. Then it would finally be over. The hand-holder was a therapist, trained in female personal crisis. She was never more than a foot from Lynn throughout that long day.

The staff was ready to go. A stainless-steel machine is

used by the doctor to vacuum it out, and the doctor needed Lynn's O.K. to begin. The whole thing was supposed to take five minutes.

Lynn got weepy from nerves, and we all waited while she collected herself. Everyone was anxious to get on with it. I bet Lynn was, too. I held her hand and kissed it; she wasn't even looking at me, she stared up at some poster on the ceiling. The sound, the way she cried, choking some, the way you do when you're sobbing lying on your back, so the spit runs down your throat, swallowing, laughing underneath the crying for how absurd the scene was— even Lynn could see it—lying there with her legs propped up in the air, all these fucking people around her holding her hands and her knees and her privates, watching her like she was—ha-ha!—about to give birth (sorry). Boo-hoo. But in my mind I keep coming back to that sound, not loud, not shrill, that crying, it was almost a noise an animal would make. How much trouble Lynn was having even crying right then, without strangling on her own spit. Is there a way to describe how much I wanted to get the fuck out of there? I wanted to shout, God of New York, turn off that sound, get me out of this room before I'm seared and split open, before I develop breasts myself. The other half of my brain, though, recorded her voice for all time.

"You're O.K.," Lynn said to nobody, to herself. "You're O.K." She'd planned to get through it without tears.

Then it was quiet and she told the doctor to go ahead,

and the doctor nodded to her assistant. The assistant turned on the machine, and the machine made a sound like any vacuum.

LYNN IS OUTSIDE, bent over the row of peas. The chicken is sitting over there in the pan. I guess it's ready to bake. She put garlic, butter, lime juice, chili powder, chopped nuts, oranges, cloves, parsley, coriander, half a banana, and paprika on it. What's left? Jean Naté? A cigar up the butt? The rice is cooking away in a pot. The chicken sits there like a drag queen, waiting to get roasted.

When it was over, Lynn went into another room and fell asleep. The therapist came over and said, "You were so caring today. Guys aren't usually so caring."

I nodded. The woman looked at me sweetly. I guess I was nice. So what. Maybe it wasn't the norm for her. Or was she just looking for a tip? My voice, though, was so much deeper than everybody else's in the room. Whatever I said that day came out sounding like a frog croak. Like a belch. My voice was unnaturally deep. I nodded as much as possible. Other than an arrest for drunk driving in college, it was the most nodding I'd ever done in one five-hour stretch.

"What are you doing?" I yell to Lynn out the window. She's bent over the rosebush. Her head is down and her shoulders are rounded, as though she's concentrating on something small.

Lynn says, "There are beetles on the roses."

I look over at the roasting pan again. "Do we cook this thing or what? I'm getting hungry. What temperature do you set it at?" No answer. She's busy with the roses.

"Lynn, you didn't turn the oven on. I'm going to come out there and pull you in by your hair."

Her hair is hanging around her face. She's looking down. "Relax," she says. "The oven is on. What time is it?" I can feel myself getting annoyed, so I take ten deep breaths, counting the numbers slowly, saying the word *relax* as I breathe out.

"Damn it, Lynn, I can't hear you." She looks up finally.

"It has to cook for an hour," she says. "And you have to move the rack."

The pan is heavier than I thought. She said move the rack. What does that mean, up or down? I grab it and then drop it, hot rack, and then the roasting pan, too, onto the oven door.

"Fuck!"

"What's going on?" she says.

"The rack is on fire."

"Of course it is, Jack, it's three hundred and fifty degrees in there. Did you burn yourself? Better put cold water on it."

I stand over the sink and let the water run on my fingers. There's a welt on my palm. I am a moron. She says, "Didn't you ever hear of an oven mitt?"

Man. My fucking hand. Did I ever hear of an oven mitt? What is that, sarcasm?

She says, "Do you want to try something weird?" Out the window I see her looking up toward me, her face flushed from leaning over for so long. "Should we put dandelions in the salad? Look at this," she says, clutching a bunch of dandelions from our lawn in a bouquet. "Mexicans kill for these, the little leaves," she says. "And they fry the flowers." I never ate dandelions before. And who cares.

"Is that too weird?" she says.

"Hey, yeah," I say, drying my burned hand gingerly on my T-shirt. "Momma had a baby and the head popped off." When I was a kid, we used to pick a dandelion and say this when we flicked the head off the stem. The water in the rice pot foams over the sides.

"Excuse me, Momma didn't have a baby and the head popped off," I say, correcting myself.

I walk over and grab a towel, move the rack down, push the chicken in, and close the oven. The door goes *spring* against the metal. It's 7:02. Nothing comes to mind. Outside she looks up at the window.

"Is that a joke?" she says.

At this angle the sun cuts right through the house. It's orange, purple, rose-colored light, blasting right through the house and spilling against everything.

"Fuck you," she says.

It's about time somebody said it. I can hear the familiar sound of it ringing in the background.

"You can never keep anything to yourself," she says.

"What?" I say.

"In your head," she says, standing at the doorway. "Forget it." Over in the rice pot, there isn't any water left. So the bottom is cooking way too fast. It's, like, black. I use a coffee cup and dump some water in. It sizzles, a cloud of steam comes up. One more cup of water. The rice starts cooking again. My eyes are tearing. In a few seconds the whole wet mess is bubbling away. I feel like I scorched my face.

Lynn's basket is overflowing with greenery and edible dandelions.

"Get out of my way," she says. "You are an animal."

"I'm sorry. Why did I say that? Is it too late to take it back?"

"What's wrong with you?" she says.

Lynn goes over to the oven with a dish towel and slides the roasting pan out. She carries it past me, not even hot yet, out the back door, and I hear it go *gong* against the metal basement doors. I step up to the window. The chicken's in the grass, onions, carrots, sliced oranges—the whole thing.

Lynn is standing in front of me now. The dish towel is wound around her hand.

"Cool," I say. "How symbolic."

She says, "I think we need therapists."

"What can I say? I'm sorry," I tell her.

"Why don't you get down on your knees."

I say, "I will if you want." No one moves.

"You're mad at me," she says. "How can you be mad at me?"

"I'm sorry. Jesus Christ. It's my fault."

She shakes her head, staring at me. "Now what?"

"I'm too hungry," I say. "I can't make any big decisions."

"What the hell happened to your face?" she says.

Outside, I pick up the roasting pan out of a pile of leaves. Lynn comes up beside me and puts the chicken back in it, and we shovel up the vegetables and carry everything over to the garbage and throw it all away, even the cracked enamel pot. Whiskey is already there at the fence, meowing and sniffing around.

"Go on, Whiskey," I say. "Not for you."

"Make sure the lid's on tight," she says to me. "I don't want to clean this up a second time from some raccoon."

LET'S SAY, FOR the sake of something, that I never loved her, that what we have here is a housing arrangement, with scenes of nude touching, that we joined for this comfort, that it's missing some key element of normal love. It's not normal, it's more like high-school love, or freshman-year-in-college kind of love, the kind you're glad to stick with as long as it doesn't interfere, as long as it doesn't start ruining your life. The very, very flawed kind. That's my idea of love, actually, those endless first two weeks, early on, when all you care about is love.

We get a pizza. We pay the man. We eat the salad she

picked and lie on the rug in the living room, eating pizza, watching TV, together on the floor. We have no furniture—we aren't there yet. The vibe between us is two people very tired and in shock, but amiable. I put some cream on my face. The welt on my hand throbs. I'd rather have pizza anyway; chicken sucks. I love her. Who else would accept me in this condition?

I should say I'll make dinner tomorrow night.

"I can make dinner tomorrow night."

"You gonna make some chicken?" she says.

"White Christmas lasagna," I say. "With spinach and salad and bread."

"Sounds good," she says. "Move over," sliding toward me. She slings her leg over both of mine, sticking her face in my neck. "This way," she says, and I move to accommodate her. I can feel Lynn's warm, clean breath on my skin. What a feeling, from one person to another.

"I don't understand anything," she says. Her eyes close. Her breath slows.

Lynn gets up from beside me and takes the dinner plates with her. I must be insane. She gives me what I need, and I love her. Hollow but true. I have to remember these things, about her and about the chicken in the grass—is that how it works? Perfect. Stupid. Shared. Turn off the TV now. Turn off the lights.

ISSUES I DEALT WITH
IN THERAPY

WE WERE ON a preppy East Coast resort island, in the middle of summer, we just flew in for the wedding of my incredible friend Bob. We were here on vacation, away from the hot city; I was so glad to be out of that fucking house. The simple fact that it's a plane trip away and you're staying in a hotel on this fake, preppy island, and because you're not married and yet you're at a wedding together, because you're too cheap to go on decent vacations, because your own day-to-day life could use some tuning up and like any sane person you've already erected an invisible barrier between yourself and that life back there and you're now pretending that it isn't real, and because Bob is suddenly this big deal, your most skyrocketing friend, and Bob's wedding weekend has finally arrived—well, it's a new beginning. I could feel the excitement.

We got to the hotel and parked the rental car and

walked down to the water in our street clothes. People passed by with beach umbrellas and L. L. Bean canvas tote bags, floating in the heat. Kids ran happily in the wet patch left by the outgoing tide as seagulls hovered rigidly in the air above us, screaming into the wind. We walked back up through the mushy sand to the steps of the hotel parking lot, Phylida's long white translucent sundress blowing in front of me. We passed the advance team for Gore, fifteen blond-haired women in their early twenties wearing hairbands talking on cell phones on the little patch of grass bordering some brown split-wood railings in front of the hotel. I was looking at everything: the people getting out of the rental cars, the bracelets on the women, the sunshine brightly beaming. It was Bob's sunshine, you were on his island now. I looked back at Phylida; she smiled. The wind lifted her dress all the way up in the front before she could catch it. A guy struggled to pull out his golf clubs from the trunk, and a valet half his age whisked the bag away like a feather. The wife laughed. Who were they? I think every room in the hotel was rented to the four hundred people invited to the wedding.

It was an old wooden hotel, the charming kind, creaking stairway, crooked floors. Our room was small, antique crap in it, a jingling glass lampshade on a side table, a queen-size bed raised to an enormous height, a frilly cover, a cheap, modern glass door on sliders leading out to a wooden balcony that gave you splinters and, as promised, looked out

on a downwind stretch of the same beach where Bob and Niloo would be getting married, a mile away.

They'd been hyping us with stuff in the mail for six months. The "Set this date aside" card. The letter that began, "Tell us exactly what you eat," with rows of boxes to check off: "Are you dairy-tolerant?" "Do you like sushi or do you eat it to be polite?" "Our chef will not cook with peanuts." The six-piece engraved invitation. Lists of the island's golf courses. A note about where they registered—"Sheetmaker to the Earl of Windsor." A special mailing to the lady guests—"We hope you'll start shopping for that perfect full-length formal summer gown to wear to our summer wedding on the shore." Another list for me because I was an usher—what kind of tux shirt collar they (Bob) wanted us to get, suggested books for preparing your toast. A sheet of facts on the island, how great Americans retired here, how it played a part in the Revolutionary War, how the something of democracy was born here—the letter Bob typed up said—"to help free our nation of tyranny evermore and make America the most wonderful country in the world."

The freak-show element of the wedding was like a side thing: Madeleine Albright would be here tomorrow; Ruth Bader Ginsburg insisted on performing the ceremony; that advance team for Gore was trying to figure out whether the rain would hold off so Al could helicopter in for an appearance.

What was I doing here?

Bob and I met during graduate school at a food drive for torture victims of repressive regimes; Bob was in charge of cans. He was silly and fun, a goofy guy in a baseball hat. He studied civil-rights law. He said he wanted to help black people straighten out the mess. I was getting a master's in international relations. Our friendship was based on leaving each other messages in fake Spanish accents, discussing girls' private areas, pretending we were rich. The next semester we became roommates. He came home at eleven o'clock and inhaled vats of popcorn.

We graduated. Bob moved out to be closer to the Justice Department. He worked in civil rights; he desegregated a poor school district in Mississippi that was secretly being run by the Klan. Bob jailed them. I sort of worshipped him. I thought he was Superman.

I worked at a nonprofit that attacked the military-industrial complex, but I'll tell you right now it did nothing. I might as well have been talking into a phone flipped upside down. It would be hard to explain exactly what we accomplished in our self-justifying fantasy of left-wing liberal dogshit.

I'd stop by and see him working and even the tiniest tic, the way his leg shook when he spoke, the way he filed papers by throwing them on the floor, seemed magnified, intentional, smart.

They won a big case and he got to be in the televised press conference. He sat up tall and straight. He'd cut his

hair short for it. Every answer out of his mouth was like a perfectly fired javelin. The camera refused to move from him. He'd starved himself on those long trips to Mississippi, and now with no hair he looked like an astronaut.

Soon he was having chats with Janet Reno, riding with her over to Congress. He wasn't lawyering as much. He'd moved up. "It's titular." What's titular? "We do planning." They had some sticky problems in Immigration and Naturalization: They were trying to figure out how to throw Haitians back in the water. When I phoned him at work he could only whisper. He gave the impression that things were hectic and constantly needed his attention. We still talked about our old plans to do good—we wanted to open a soup kitchen in a motor home and drive it around—but he liked seeing himself on the news, and the next time we were together he did a long analysis reworking the performance I saw on TV. He went to events at the White House, standing in for the attorney general. "After Memorial Day," he explained, "you wear the white dinner jacket."

Time passed. He met everybody. He called Barbara Walters at her home. He had four thousand names in his handheld electronic Rolodex. I swung by his apartment. He stuck handwritten notes from King Hussein on his refrigerator, photos of himself coming down the staircase of *Air Force One*, looking pale and tired. He'd become important, and I was hypnotized and gladly took what he handed me, a box of candies, an opened bottle of peach schnapps, outpourings of guilt he felt at the sight of me.

He quit Justice and went to work on a guy's campaign. He ran it and won. You saw Bob on TV on election night, dancing in a hat he made out of a dinner napkin. He became a "media catastrophe consultant"—what's that? He "befriended politicians under fire." He sat in on meetings. Alone, just the two of us, he entertained me with their indiscretions: the congressman accused of photocopying his testicles, the federal judge who fell into fetal position when women said no. He needed somebody to be his friend, to help him grasp what he'd become, but I also got the feeling he went in and out of remembering I was there.

He bought a nice house. He got a smaller cell phone, a full-time squirrelly assistant cutting into our lunches to tell Bob he had to go. He went to work for Senator Sheslow, whose wife had just had a stroke, she was an invalid; Sheslow thought he might run for president. Bob was flying to Dallas and Japan, talking to folks. "It's like fund-raising." And Al Gore was calling to consider him for a job. These jobs didn't have names anymore. "I'll be the youngest member of Gore's top guys," he told me in his monotone robotic rambling into the speaker phone as he drove alone somewhere, exhausted. "It'll be outstanding," he said.

He had other distinctions. A booming voice, big hands, thick fingers, brown-colored dents on his car from backing into trees, pouchy bags under his bloodshot eyes, a colossal memory—he could produce anything ever said in passing, the name of my childhood pet turtle, how Sheslow voted

on a tax bill fifteen years before, it all sat front row in his mind, it was all immediate. He knew Bill Bradley's weak spots, the trajectory of Chinese rocketry. He had constant weight problems. He shrunk and ballooned and went on diets. He was hungry. He kept popcorn in a lunch bag in his suit-coat pocket. He bit his fingernails till they bled like they'd been shoved inside a sink disposal. I felt for him, but he didn't need my sympathy. I'd wonder, What's he going to do next? Why did he like me? Why was Bill Clinton calling this guy for advice when he couldn't park his car without hanging two wheels on the curb?

The way he spoke now had changed; he used the word *outstanding*, the word *sequentially*. The last time I saw him was at this brunch fund-raiser he made me go to; he'd been bingeing on wheat-grass pills for four days and had stomach cramps and diarrhea but he said he felt "fantastic." And the way he acted now—in the last year and a half he went from a young power-hungry sellout to, like, my uncle Denny with the fat gut and the sweaty sheen, wetting his shirts, singing corny show tunes into my answering machine. "I'm sorry I called at such a late hour, the next time I do I'll bring you a flower."

Seeing him, the rare times I got together with him now, passing by his office at the Capitol, stopping at his house to be yawned at, or snored at, was like visiting his grave. Niloo would watch his snoring nostrils—he looked like a gorilla—and go, "He flies pretty high, doesn't he?" or

"Guess who phoned us last night." In the old days I could get up and go home. Now I had to listen to his bullshit from her too, swallow it twice.

PHYLIDA AND I stepped out on the balcony. White-painted wicker chairs with cushions, a table warped by weather, suspended on three legs. Two guys stood on the balcony next to ours, doing what we were doing, feeling the air. They were Italians, friends of Bob and Niloo's, also just arrived. Both guys were tan, had facial hair, wore mirrored lenses. They'd changed into swimming stuff and were ready to go down to the beach. They looked like a couple. One guy wore a very fine loosely woven shiny multicolor sweater in the zillion-degree sun. He fingered his webbed beach purse. The other guy had clean-shaven legs which were flawless and brown. The guy with the purse said, "We met them vacationing at a place like this in Lisbon." He said this to the air in front of him. I had a panicky urge to figure out when Bob and Niloo had been to Lisbon, but I couldn't picture what continent Lisbon was on so I said, "What kind of place was that?" Both guys smiled at once. I'd been holding Phylida's hand, and brought it up and kissed it.

On the balcony on the other side a woman sat alone having a beer on her wicker loveseat. Her name was Sebastian. She had a long, washed-out-green dress unwrinkling on a hanger, and the ocean breeze kept tipping it into her face as she sat, looking pale and basically dead, squinting

into the hot sun reflecting off the ocean. Phylida leaned across the railing and asked, "Did you and Niloo grow up together in New Jersey?" Sebastian knew Niloo from college. She offered Phylida a beer. Already, the first lonely person Phylida saw she befriended. The gay guys stood muscularly in belted swim trunks. I went back inside and hung up my suit.

I lay down on the bed and listened to the women chat. They told each other where they'd come from. Phylida worked into her intro that Bob and I no longer knew each other. Sebastian said, "I can't believe I got invited to this thing." Phylida was leaning on the balcony divider, moving her weight back and forth, her butt aimed at the opening in the doorway at my feet. I felt myself relaxing. Phylida's butt had become the focal point of our life together. It was soft and circular and amazing. I wanted to crawl inside it. I got comfort knowing it was there. She was explaining her medical residency to Sebastian. Now it was swinging. I shut my eyes and began twitching, conking out like the over-worked dead person with foul breath I'd become.

After a while Phylida came in and closed the sliding glass door and the see-through curtain, not the heavier, room-darkening drape, and lay down next to me and explained that Sebastian hadn't rented a car and wanted to ride over with us to the rehearsal dinner. Then she fell asleep. She hadn't slept all week. She hadn't slept in seven months and four years. Medical residents are sleep-deprived. On call for three surgical rotations this week, she

slept through her beeper one night, what they call a "no-hitter," got clobbered the next two nights with huge repair jobs, came home in a black cloud, unable to talk.

I said, "Are you asleep?" She didn't move. "How can somebody name a girl Sebastian?"

Phylida and I never fought. We also never saw each other. Our life consisted of lengths of days, with nothing fun in the middle, grinding. We got together and listed what had happened since the last time we spoke, became sad and fell asleep. I kissed her canted hipbone. I ran my finger along her "zipper," the scar that went from her sternum to her crotch, open heart surgery as a kid, what got her interested in medicine back then, coarctation of the aorta—a narrow, collapsing aorta, congenitally smushed. I weighed her chest. She let me. I said, "Should I let you sleep?"

She said, "Did I sleep on the plane?" I said yes. She turned toward me exhaling. "This'll be us someday."

"What?"

"You and me."

Phylida and I were on the verge of something. Picture us picturing ourselves as next in line for our own wedding weekend. (We'd already talked about what kind of ring I would get her—the stone, the setting.) Picture us wondering: Why does this feel like nothing? Picture us thinking the same thing separately and not talking about it and coming up empty. She was trying to be nice, waiting for that

fucking ring now for months and months; she did this imi-
tation of an adoring girlfriend, holding my Coke in the car,
but it made her furious and we both wanted to get this
over with.

I went for her chest, unbuttoning as fast as I could,
opening up her bra. She looked in my eyes and waited.

I ran my hands all over her body. Phylida let out a
breath and smiled. Her flaxen hair fell in a spiral shape
across a pillow. I kissed her nipples. She liked that. She did
a noise with her tongue against her teeth—*tchk*—as I
moved my hands around her silky cream mountains. I'd al-
ways been attracted to her, although sometimes she walked
down the street like John Wayne with his dungarees shoved
up his ass in *Stagecoach*.

"They're yours," she said.

"What is?"

"This is the last pair of tits you'll ever squeeze," she said,
and giggled.

"Why do you have to talk as if you just got out of an in-
sane asylum?" I said. She smiled. Why didn't I understand
where she was going with any particular thought?

I licked her ribs. She took her dress off. She had a face
that held all the mysteries of Ireland. She had a single
blond hair coming out of her chin I never saw before. She
wore old blue cotton panties with just a slight fume of
musk and salt. She let me pull them all the way down. She
had a cunt. It was pink and cunt-shaped and smelled like

roses. What else? She had a mother and a father. Her mother was the garden-variety kind, antihistamines, uppers, soda can in the hand, surprising cotton-ball-white pageboy hairdo. Her father left the family every year on Christmas; he mailed us refrigerator-size boxes of furniture out of guilt. She made a bubble noise in her sleep. She lived for running late; she drove fast, ran people over in crosswalks. She smelled like saddle soap. She had a cowlick on her forehead. She had microscribbled blue capillaries beneath the furry softness on the back of her neck. Her hair looked like corn silk. Her lips were a cornfield. She lay between the rows of corn on the bedspread and let me touch her and wanted more.

"I like that," she said, pulling at me.

It terrified me when she acted like a slut. I said, "Let me get unbuckled."

Bob's fantastic wedding weekend, plane ride from Boston, dry in-flight peanuts, mysterious hotel on the ocean, the grooved tracks of nauseating similarities between us and every other person in this hotel, in the world.

I stared at her. I wanted to get married, too. I wanted to be swept away. Phylida and I had talked about our whole lives—where to live, how to live; we met the other's family, everybody loved everybody, yabba blabba—the only thing left was, like, pull the trigger, get that ring!

She said, "Your winky is starting to get a little small." She said this in a bright voice, ashamed of herself. She held

it at the base—the outline of her lips was white—and tried blowing me.

I could feel myself spiraling away from sex toward all my fears and anxieties. I tried to "get metaphysical" with my fears, to keep with my psychologist's urging (she, of the fluffy, Native American "dream catcher" on her gray office wall) so they didn't overtake me. I looked down at Phylida, beautifully pumping away, and the face of Steven Spielberg floated into my mind, expressionless, bearded, dumb-founded. I thought of how much money he had. He had a private jet with customized woodwork interior, a daybed with a nightstand and a cup holder. A friend of Bob's, some jackass named Dan who helped me plan the order of who gave what toasts this weekend, also had a private jet. Shares of Dan's amazing start-up company cost twenty-six cents apiece two years ago. At this moment they're worth forty-seven dollars. Some of the other invitees were in on Dan's first stock offering; they had names like Lafayette and Sky. I didn't have enough money to be showing my face around this crowd. Sometimes when I traveled for work I pretended I was a foreign spy. I wasn't a spy. Dan would be arriving in his jet today; in a half hour, in fact. I knew that because Bob once suggested I pick Dan up with my personal chauffeuring services but I actually wouldn't be able to because Dan could go fuck himself.

What was with the old, baggy, stained underwear Phylida wore? They looked like something from a nursing

home. And what about that chin hair? What about the Italian woman in my office with the extremely high-heeled black suede boots, who did this little secret cha-cha with her legs whenever she came and stood by my desk?

Phylida. If there was any way on earth for me to make her happy, make her laugh, make her feel better, I would find it. But I didn't love her. Not a little. Nothing. I didn't *not* love her. This had nothing to do with love. This was a life arrangement, for all time. What could that mean? Being married forever, living in timeless eternity. Not a joyous eternity, not that basketball-shaped baloney with no ends—slice and slice and there's still a ton left—but the other eternity of Christian-fundamentalist kooks, floating around dead in a pink nightie with a dopey look on your face and a gold banjo, trying to be good.

Happiness. Half penis. I didn't have the slightest interest in fooling around.

I pushed Phylida off me. She looked up, smiling, trying to keep the mood upbeat. Her red mouth, her beautiful face. I would've liked to chop my dick off and fling it from the balcony. "It's not gonna work," I said.

"Don't get hysterical."

"It happened last week. That's twice in a row."

"It happens to you every time we try to have sex away from home." That placid look, that flat-lipped smile. She touched her lips. Her eyelashes were like a foot long. They flapped through the air. Her eyes sparkled so wet and clear and blue like the soaring heart of Bob's tumescent sky

groaning with sunlight outside our windows that I had to stop looking or die. Why do married people have to live together in our society? Why can't they get houses next door to each other, shoot semen through the window? Why did she like to kick me in her sleep? Why did I feel like strangling her flutelike pinkish throat when she did?

I said, "I fucked you in Mexico."

"You fucked me in Mexico."

"Right."

"Don't get all penis-focused."

"Could we not talk about it and make me feel even worse?"

"You're thinking about getting married, our life together. You're worried about eternity."

"I'm not thinking about anything."

"You're still my hero. I believe in you."

"Oh Christ."

"I'm trying to help."

I stood, wearing just my underwear, and walked to the bathroom.

"You're rushing. You're tired."

"Thank you."

"You have a wedgie."

The bathroom had a full set of amenities in a wicker basket packed in tissue paper. French soap in a plastic case, English shampoo, a thing to shine shoes. I felt humiliated. A highly detailed advertisement for blackheads stared back at me. I ran some water. I heard her speaking to someone

about her outfit for tonight. "It's blue and it has an A line." I couldn't hear what else she said. She giggled.

"What's so funny?"

"I'm telling my mother how fat I look in my dress." I gargled with the complimentary mouthwash and went back out. Phylida lay naked, propped on the bed and put her hand over the receiver.

"My mother said the problem is in your mind and you have nothing to worry about." Ha! Good one! She switched from me back to the phone to me again and said, "She said I should get you some of those pills and you'll be fine." I thought she was kidding. She said good-bye.

"Was there really somebody on the other end?"

"Relax," she said. "Anyway, that medication's not what it's cracked up to be."

"Is that what you told your mother?"

"It's a joke. Lighten up. We're on vacation." She said something about absorption problems inhibiting blood flow. "Worse-case scenario, science can do things for this now." She looked at me with her earnest bullshit doctor face. She started dialing another number.

"Hang up the phone."

"I have to check my messages." She rested the phone on her pubic bone. "There's a procedure; they make a two-millimeter incision at the base of the phallus and slide a lubricated sterile tube inside. It explodes and stiffens when you activate the prosthetic device." Phylida was in the

surgery unit in her residency and showed real talent for it and liked the ability to both scalpel living people and pretend to be saving them.

"You don't mean *explode*," I said. "That word would be *expand*." I didn't want anyone exploding my dick.

"They implant a piece of polyethylene, it's an outpatient procedure—and it can be filled with either sterile salt water or air, I believe."

"Are you dialing direct?"

"Why?"

"Because hotels rip you off."

"You're not the boss of my money." She sat there, now sadly looking at the neatly spiraled phone cord lying along her small flat belly, the phone covering her nice vagina.

PHYLIDA PLACED HER makeup bag on the bed, ready to go. She looked like a suffocating powdered mannequin. I felt the same but looked worse. Sebastian knocked and came in and stood by the television cabinet. She'd somehow found a greenish eye shadow to match her dress, and the added touches of it along her cheekbones made her face look skinless. With the acne and veins visible on her arms, she radiated pulsing green blood. On closer inspection she smelled of sour panic sweat. I smiled at her and she touched her jaw.

Phylida read the premailed directions ("Unscheduled toasts may come after dessert and coffee") as I drove

through town to the restaurant. Every inch of street was jammed with traffic and sunburned people in salmon-colored shorts shoving past each other, licking melting ice cream off their wrists. Sebastian talked nonstop: "I wonder if Bibbity Blob is coming." She talked about Niloo's college days: "She bought a new purse every time she went to New York City. She slept with what's-his-name." When we pulled in line for the car valet, Sebastian asked if I had a tissue and cleared her throat and served up a morsel of vomit. "I hate this kind of thing," she said. Phylida leaned backward with her arm through the slit in the front seats, the dark-blue matte cloth of her dress pulling taut across her front, highlighting her individuated teardrop-shaped braless tits that I'd felt before, and patted Sebastian's knee.

The women walked behind me as I strode through the restaurant, trying to think of a way to tell people I'd been to London twice for work in the last six months. There was a patio where people stood drinking. The dining area was out back under a tent. We said hello to Bob's parents and met Niloo's parents, Mr. and Mrs. Niyangoda, and Mr. Niyangoda's new wife, Naomi. Phylida looked around and said it all seemed nice, and I nodded and she said, "At my wedding the bridesmaids will wear metallic scarves, very little makeup, full-length illusion skirts. The cake will be made to look like Wedgewood."

Sebastian was wondering what Niloo's hair would be like. Sebastian's own hair was short and so greasy and frail it looked like it had been waxed to her head. Something

about events like these made people appear either acceptable or pathetic. I got us another round. I'd actually had one more up at the bar, which made three. Was my drinking maybe becoming something? Had it blossomed over these last few months, at home at night, waiting for Phylida, alone until 2 or 3 A.M., foggy and secretly seething? It was a question.

Phylida and Sebastian moved off to find food. A man with a foreign accent came up to me and said I was not to worry: even though he'd lost ten million dollars when he consolidated his businesses, the former premier of France was on his new executive board. He then drank his drink, said nothing, and stared at me. Another man joined us, holding a cigarette. His face had fine lines like an apple going soft. He said he thought the island was beautiful. People chatted. An older woman pulled on the skin of her throat and said, "I'm going to have this done." At the other end of the lawn I spotted Phylida chewing; her mouth was full and she waved her hand furiously through the air at me in an exaggerated gleeful way—there was no sorrow in her jaw. I didn't have the money to marry that girl. Originally I liked her because she looked dumb. I didn't know she was a doctor. She swam some delicacy in front of her mouth to taunt me before popping it, and a bullfrog bellowed sadly nearby, similar to the noise my dad made when he let one go; my heart felt like an anvil, it was pulling me down.

Candles were being lit inside the tent. I picked up the scent of pipe tobacco and gardenias. The moon came out. I

spotted Bob in a blue tie and red silk pocket square and a straw-colored coat that was already damply dark under the arms and along the back from sweat. The last time I spoke to him was three months earlier when he left me waiting at a Thai restaurant until I gave up, because on the way over Sheslow beeped him. "Well," he said. The deep voice. He shook hands with everyone and then gave me a slap on the back, a broad, thick hand with rock-hard fingers kneading into my trapezius muscle like it was about to tear it off the bone. He sucked in air. "It's terrific to see you."

"Yeah?"

"Come with me."

I wondered if Bob was taking me aside to explain why he'd chosen me as an usher and to give me a Tiffany sterling-silver fountain pen with my initials. I wondered if maybe he was flipping out and needed to talk seriously right now about marrying Niloo. He pulled out a set of keys. The sky was dusky and you could see fireflies.

He said, "My father-in-law brought some wine in his car. Would you just give me a hand?"

As we looked for the car in an open field beside the patio I reminded Bob we hadn't spoken in months. He tried to remember our last talk. "I'm at a loss," he said, smiling. He asked me about work.

I shifted my coat and nothing occurred to me. I shrugged.

"Don't worry." He laughed, and hit me again; Bob language for trying to be reassuring. "It'll get better." For such

an unfeeling, pompous dick, he'd often come through with ways to help—calling an editor at the op-ed page of the *Times,* introducing me to a scientist at one of his campaign fund-raisers who later testified for us on the Hill. He'd actually spent hours of his spare time last winter finding a job for one of our interns who wanted to work as a legislative aide. Why?

"Where do you go for your honeymoon?" I asked.

"A tiny island nation near Sri Lanka." He said he knew the king.

As we got to the trunk of Mr. Niyangoda's black Mercedes I noticed that Bob's sweat stains had spread up to his chest below his chin.

How was *his* work going?

"Fantastic." This was the most incredible week of his life. He put his finger in my face: "Sheslow will be the next president of the United States. I have no doubt." They'd just been tacitly endorsed by this one slob, things were zooming. "We will make our nation strong and safe, and ethnic violence will be eradicated by prosperity." He was going on C-SPAN on Monday. His shirt collar pinched his neck just slightly, so an arc of flesh hung from his chin. "We're bringing slot machines to highway rest stops."

I said, "How does C-SPAN decide—"

He grabbed his beeper and called in to work while I listened to the tones of his tiny flip phone, waiting.

No word yet from Gore. "If he comes tomorrow," he said, "I've got the job."

What about the senator's presidency? I asked.

"Staying where I am would be a lateral move." He thought more and said, "In my heart I know he's a freak."

I said, "Bob, you're going to the White House."

He said, "I can't believe my life!" He was so excited he dropped the keys on the ground trying to open the lock.

In the trunk there were four cases of wine. The cases were made of wood. He said, "Do you know about *premier cru*?" He gave it his disgusting French accent. He lifted one up and read the name off the box. "Stuff like this goes right to the collectors," he said. He slid the case toward me on the lip of the trunk and sighed, grinning widely as the light from the restaurant caught the sheen off his temples, and whispered, "I feel like a god right now, you know?"— he was having a kind of galaxial moment—as the case began falling between us like some terrible tipped boulder and we both lunged for it, trying to stop it with our knees, and failing, as it slipped down the bumper, and there was a miserable gnashing of sound, the unmistakable sound of glass breaking.

Bob came up with his teeth set across his open mouth. I froze. "Are you crazy?" he said.

I said, "You had it."

"You're such an idiot," he said. He tore a panel off the top of the crate and very carefully checked each bottle, setting them neatly on the grass. The neck of one was cracked beneath the foil and the top came off when he touched it, gushing wine. "Convenient twist-off," he said, staring at me

insanely. He poured the rest on the grass in front of me and turned and fired the bottle out of sight. It went through some trees and smashed.

"That's five hundred dollars," he said. "It's a lot of money for a guy like you to be wasting."

I pointed to the red stain on his blazer. I couldn't stop myself.

"Oh no," he said. "Look at my—look at my coat!" He held his elbow up in the air and then spotted his shirt cuff, also stained. "You got my cuff, too!" In fact, I hadn't spilled anything anywhere. My gaze fell to the ground—but there, on his shoes—

"My Cole Haan! You got it on my shoe!" We both reached down at the same time to wipe the wine off his *leche*-colored shoe and banged heads. He stood up, going loony now, gripping his brow, and in the split second in which he appeared to be deciding whether to punch me out or laugh, he suddenly poked me in the head with his nail-hard poking finger and said, "That's using the old noggin!" He went on, trying to be as lighthearted and fun as possible. "Your brain," he said, searching for something clever, "is like the surface of Mars, a red rocky place where scientists believe there is life"—he kept poking, poke poke—"But there's no life, right?" They had not yet found life on Mars, yes, I had to agree. Then he laughed and shook me as though the whole thing was a joke: "You almost wasted a case worth six thousand dollars!" I laughed, too. I try to laugh as much as possible.

• • •

WHEN I GOT back to the tent, I spotted Phylida waving a seating card at me. The banquet had been divided into sections named after the countries of antiquity. We were in Flanders. Next over was Gaul, then Mesopotamia.

Phylida's face was flushed deep bluish red, as she gestured toward Sebastian, "We've been glugging too much." Sleep deprivation combined with the many substances that swam inside her—she'd self-prescribed medications for everything from dry inner-eyelid lining to mood swings to clenched jaw muscles—along with drinking a gallon of wine made her brain tilt slightly, causing her to combine or invent words. Sebastian held a stricken, catlike pose. Then she left, having been assigned to Bavaria.

Appetizers arrived. Bob's dad gave the first speech, and I felt a funny gurgle down inside me like a warm gastric balloon rising. From that moment on, each time someone stood up, I experienced a slight cramping gut, kind of needing to poop, while assembling and abandoning thoughts for the toast I was about to give; I'd feel in my pocket for the notes I'd made on the plane in case my speech flopped; then the speaker would finish and the balloon would—deflate.

I said to Phylida, "Can you see a mark on my forehead?" She shrugged, but I felt it; it stung where he'd doinked me as if he was doinking me still.

She said, "I'm sunburned." She put her hand on the bare skin above the scooped-out back of her dress and made a

red flash burn. Ouch. She'd sat out on the porch at the height of the afternoon with Sebastian, bare-shouldered in her flimsy sundress, while I napped.

Bob's brother made a toast.

A bird flew into the tent and got trapped. It came closer, pounding the air above me. I seemed to be the only one who noticed. My colon felt distended. Dan, the guy with his own private jet, was standing at the microphone, his glass raised. "They are today's dream, tomorrow's hope." It sounded like an illiterate campaign speech. But the toast that followed Dan's was worse. I racked my brain to think of something to say to two hundred people. I burped, and it smelled like an egg that had turned rotten.

Suddenly Phylida pulled both shoulders of her dress down and put some ice from the butter dish on her neck. When I asked what was going on she said, "My wine's completely dranken. Drinken." She had a selective intelligence. She looked around. "We need the guy." I waved at him. Maybe it was simply the release after so much hard work at the hospital. Without the support of the shoulder straps, her tits suddenly shuddered and fell down. "Hello," my girlfriend-slash-fiancée-slash-bulb-headed alien then said to the folks across from us. "I already got a hangover."

Why was everything starting to suck?

I studied the face of Wayne, Bob's closest longtime buddy, as he carefully picked his way along Bob's first kiss in summer camp, their car accident in drivers' ed, how glad but also sorry he was to see Bob getting hitched.

Bob stood and toasted Niloo, a "great great person." She sat looking up at him uncomfortably as he spoke. "How on earth do you put up with me?"

He had, I now realized, completely accepted his fate: to go through life as a humorless douchebag for whom everything came too easily. He showed no sign of effort, his voice broke, he paced himself. "This woman," he said, "is the love of my life."

Phylida was now sweating. I said, "What's wrong with you?"

She said, "When is this gonna end?" She said she'd slept four hours total since Wednesday (though that didn't count drooling all down her blouse on the airplane) and started telling me about the last patient she'd admitted this morning, a homeless guy. She said there's a certain kind of fungus that only grows on a person's anus, and he had it. It eats skin. She gave me her saintly look of pain.

I said, "You knew this would be a late night," and she started to cry. She put her hand up to her throat and took her pulse and put the other hand in the middle of her chest.

She said, "I'm having an arrhythmic palpitation." Her kind of aortic problem had been fixed with surgery. This was only a murmur. She started tapping her cheek.

"What are you doing?"

"It's a test for hypocalcemia."

I said, "Call a taxi. Just go." She said she had to wait until I made my toast.

Niles was solemnly reading the exact figures of the landslide election Bob won running for seventh-grade class president from the original newspaper he'd saved when a woman in the seat next to me looked over and sighed. I smiled back—I was next. On the far end of the tent guys were talking very loudly, smoking cigarettes. The gay guys from the hotel balcony pressed by, saying *ciao*. It was almost eleven. Phylida wasn't the only one with her head on the table. People were croaking. We'd all traveled a long way today, flown to this island, and we'd toasted and drunk. The woman introduced herself—she was actually seated in Gaul and had to lean over because of the gap between tables.

I hadn't seen her before. I said, "You're a friend of Niloo's?" She said no. Her name was Anne. I said, "How do you know Bob?"

"He's a new friend."

"What does that mean?"

Leaning toward me caused the front of her dress to fall open; the tops of her tits were tanned and between her white-satin bra cups was a tiny miniature bow the size of a snowflake, and I wondered if some person had tied that bow by hand. "Actually I work for Gore."

I said, "Oh." She nodded. I said, "Were you with that group by the hotel this afternoon?"

She said, "I work on his senior staff in fund-raising." Across the tent Niles was winding up. My gut bubbled.

"Is Al coming tomorrow?" She didn't know. Her dress

was white with black S-shaped vines across the front. A sizeable chunk of her tit came exposed when she moved her arm. In order not to stare I looked down at my hands meditatively, but the glow of her high-cut panties came through the body-hugging front of her dress. I said, "Are you going to hire Bob?"

She said, "We think he's amazing."

People had been saying that all night. I still couldn't figure out what they meant. "Like what parts, exactly?"

"His intelligence, his loyalty, his experience, his values." She had the serious determination of a nine-year-old girl burning army ants with a match.

"Yeah?"

"We admire his belief system."

Belief system? Based on what—liking people with money? The great wines of Burgundy? Gorging himself on chicken tikka masala and then sticking his finger down his throat in the restaurant parking lot and puking between the headlights of my car? The belief system that let him zip money into a certain fund during his last campaign from this other giant account ("A gift, really, from a very dear friend") out of which he paid himself?

"Oh," I said. "What belief system?"

Phylida, meanwhile, had woken up. I'm not sure how long she'd been staring at me. My future soul mate–slash–fever blister–slash–sleeping beauty had a string bean imprinted on her cheek. With her giant eyes and her pink face she looked like an unborn squirrel.

I said, "This is Anne."

Phylida said, "Did you enjoy looking down her dress?"

People cheered. Niles was done.

I took forever pushing between chairs to get to the spot with the mike. My legs felt like two thick rusty chains. I tested the microphone. There was suddenly an audience, staring.

I took out the note in my pocket and silently read it. The night Bob phoned, in tears, about leading the polls. Hmm. I paused solemnly. Bob rose up in his chair and keyed in on me. He had that stupid set to his eyes and mouth—picture Donald Trump—of always waiting to be looked at. I gazed over the crowd. What I was going to say? "Well." The skin of my face felt like it had been stretched on a coat hanger in front of an oven that was my head. The next line on the piece of paper said, "Story about landlady." I thought for a second. It was something about a pizza box catching fire on the stove.

I cleared my throat. My legs: heavy. My face: hot. I thought of FDR, the late-afternoon stiffness in his joints, the onset of polio. I sputtered. "You've had a lot of jobs, Bob." I really should've read this over on the plane.

"Quite a few." I couldn't speak. "Big jobs." There's no funny or clever metaphor for what I was failing to do up there. I had lost my air of assumed normalness. I should've figured I'd flip out and written down every word. I was dying. I wanted to sit. I gritted my teeth and clenched my ass up and tried to go forward. "You're smart." I couldn't

breathe. "Very smart." My small lungs shot puffs of white gas—performance anxiety. "An incredible guy." The people closest to me looked as if an asteroid was coming over my shoulder and about to crush them. "Unfortunately, I'm blanking on some of your successes." A couple of the smokers were laughing at me. Well, wouldn't you? "I'm sure they'll come to me in a moment." I reached down and quietly drank an entire glass of water. "Why couldn't I have been at some loser's wedding now?" I said, to myself, out loud, into the microphone. "I wouldn't have to remember so much." Bob's head looked like a fire engine, his nostrils flaring, and his glare made the noise of a fire engine horn. Niloo was grinning. "Can't you stop and give somebody else a chance, for Christ's sake?" I put the water down and gripped the mike stand. I'm going to faint, I thought. No. I'm going to explode from my bowels. And then I'll faint.

It began as a queasy chuckle or two, and then the entire room erupted in a wave of laughter. In fact they'd been laughing for a while. All night everyone had been dying just to crack a smile—the natural tendency is to want to laugh at events like this—but no one had given them a chance. Now they had me: the buffoon. I pulled the mike from the stand and reached up to wipe the sweat off my face and they laughed at that too, the most uproarious laugh so far. What the hell?

"Anyway, standing up here talking to you," I said, feeling more confident suddenly, "is actually the most time we've spent together in a year and a half, you big pain

in the ass." They roared like a beer-hall crowd as Bob watched me, and I found myself remembering him working his cell phone earlier in the night, and pictured shoving it down his throat with a toilet plunger. The smokers had joined in, they were yelling at Bob now, mocking me; one called him a pain in the ass. I stepped forward, trying to keep the momentum with me, and said, "After Bob moves to the Oval Office," pointing to them, "he'll send you guys some interns." More yuks, far out of proportion to the dopiness of the joke. I raised my right hand and in a lame Clinton drawl said, "I, Bob, solemnly swear to set aside interns who can suck a bowling ball through a Krazy Straw for my dearest former roommate." They yelled. Niloo had leaned into Bob's shoulder, she had her hand over her mouth, her face was twisted frozen as she cracked up. I made one of those fists politicians use when they're trying to be emphatic. Niloo couldn't control herself. I said, "Is this funny to you, Niloo? Do you know what you're in for?" Her face was crimped and she was sort of nodding. "Can I give you some advice?" I paused—why had I been screaming?—and continued, quietly this time. "Stand up and start running and never look back."

I began shaking my head cornily. "You're a nice person, Niloo. It's such a shame." More hilarity, a monsoon. "But if you're going to live your life together"—I started doing a bad televangelist Southern idiot—"you must never stand directly in front of him after he has eaten a large meal. It's very dangerous. And do not worry your pretty self about

his latest diet, O.K.?" I made a puking, retching motion. "Don't be surprised if he sticks his finger down his throat and throws up all over your car." I took a breath and pointed at him. "I don't know if anybody told you, Bob, vomiting and diarrhea are not the best answer to weight gain." I was on autopilot. "Try Richard Simmons's *Sweatin' to the Oldies*." I did a little dance move. People were really letting go now; one guy slipped out of his chair and a waiter had to dodge him. Bob was staring at me, immobile, his large mind turning.

Bob wasn't going to be introducing me to Al Gore tomorrow.

Over in Flanders, Phylida bent over suddenly and the people seated by her jumped backward out of their chairs. Phylida, I realized, had either just thrown up or had knocked something over or had fallen comatose onto the ground. That's my woman. I was marrying Drankenstein. I was the bride of Drankenstein. What a wonderful couple we'd make. How fun we were at a party. What a future we had. Phylida reared her head after a moment, eyeballs rolling high into her forehead, with her sweaty brownrooted old hair plastered against it, and I imagined my being up here again—next year? the summer after?—toasting her at our own wedding, and I thought: I might as well kill myself. "Bob," I said, and waited for his expression to change. No change. He was looking at me like I was a stain on your carpet that you scrubbed and it got worse. Ah, what the hell. I raised my empty glass and the place got

silent. "How come you never call me back anymore, you fat, pusillanimous, popcorn-eating, obsequious, spermy, whoring, curry-barfing ass licker?"

Had I gone too far?

"That," Phylida said, looking up at me when I returned to the table, her face gaunt and sculpted, "was a disaster."

I said, "We can go now." The party started breaking up then. We stood and got ready to leave.

Anne opened her mouth wide and laughed when our eyes met. "That was quite a testimonial," she said. "What else do you know about Bob?" I felt a haze, like mucus, covering my eyes. I watched her as she stood and moved closer, clearly excited.

"What else do I know?"

She had one of those high waists with hips that were just a bit too wide so her dress sat up there like a slipcover hanging on a sofa pillow. "Tell us something really juicy." I thought I'd said enough.

BACK AT THE hotel, Phylida pulled her dress up over her head and threw it in the corner under the desk, kicked her shoes off, pulled down her nylons, and sat on the edge of the bed in her underwear, groaning. Even hunched over like that, there wasn't a blip of fat on her. She put on her spaghetti-strap camisole. I stared at her long torso, her strong shoulders, her long neck. She looked like she was made out of rubber. I waited for her to look at me. "Are you gonna go right to sleep?" I said.

I was trying to be nice, trying not to want her. The night's debacle had left me charged. Why was her arm skin so soft? We were here together in this perfect glimpse of unreal time in a fancy hotel, and I wanted to keep it that way. I looked at her and she yawned, which made her shiver so her tits shuddered. "I'm going to bed." She was so beautiful our whole life threatened to devolve into my headless worship of her hot beauty. My dick, of course, was hard. Not like that egg-yolk dick from earlier today. It now lay in my pants like a stunned fish. I loved her so much I couldn't think. I loved her because I was horny. I was horny because I was sad, because the night had been awful, because it was almost over. I thought back to that shocked look on Bob's face during my toast, the crowd laughing all around him.

"I thought we might go down to the beach," I said. She looked in her makeup bag and got out some pills. She threw them down dry and pulled out her sleep mask from her makeup bag. She shook the strap out.

"I love you," I said. I asked her if she wanted to take her top off. She put the mask on her head. The sound of my voice was deep and nasal, the way it had been when it carried across the crowd, amplified, when it shook the crowd.

"O.K.," she said. She pulled my hand off her arm. "Don't touch me."

"That's it?"

"You're wired about your toast. You feel like you put one over on Bob, don't ask me why." She lay back on top of the

bedspread and pulled her eye mask down. Her panties were whisper-weight, see-through orange lace. I put my nose next to her foot and sniffed it. I pictured giving it to her as she bit me and seizured and sobbed, loving it. I felt so released after all that worrying—so overjoyed. I pictured ramming that wine bottle up Bob's ass, breaking off the shattered stem while he's whooping and screaming. I pictured Richard Nixon getting shot, red wine splashing, trying to hold the lapels of his suit closed as he fell. I saw Bill Clinton, floating in space, docking headfirst into the space station. She lifted the edge of her mask and looked at me for a long moment with one eye. "If you want to do it," she said, "go ahead."

I thought for a second. Something about it seemed wrong. "Forget it." She pulled the mask back down and moved her nose once and was gone.

I found Sebastian out on her wicker loveseat. I climbed over the partition and sat next to her. The smell of her in the moonlight. I smelled pee; late-night sour wine breath? I don't know, something bitter—mixed with sweat. She was smoking a cigarette and said she came a long way not to talk to anybody the whole night. She said Niloo's other college friends had been seated together, away from her. "They see each other anyway because they all live in Boston." She had an elbow on her knee with the cigarette in that hand; it looked like she'd done this position most nights. She said the trip cost her a thousand dollars. Her lips jutted out stiffly when she tried to smoke. It wasn't just

the pee-pee smell that made talking to her so tricky. She was unsure and furious about the whole world around her. (On top of everything else, in my haste to get Phylida back to our room, we'd ditched Sebastian and I didn't know how she'd gotten back.) I wanted to say to her, "What did you expect?" She looked at me, shaking her head with her mouth open, and ran out of gas. She tried again, "Do you think she intended for me not to come?" A steady drip fell from the balcony above us, from a wet bathing suit. I said no. The moonlight caught her eyelashes and from here she looked like a lonesome, long-nosed, greasy teenage boy. There was so little moonlight I couldn't figure out what her face was doing. I said, "You don't have to invite her to yours."

Her arm that had been propped on her knee fell into her her lap, and her head went to that angle the librarian's would go to when I stopped at the med school and asked if she'd seen Phylida. She said, "Invite her to my what?"

"What?"

She said, "You're so fucking lucky you got somebody else. You're so lucky." She was waiting to take another puff.

What did I have to say about that?

PHYLIDA LAY ON her side on the bedspread in her underwear, the table lamp on beside her. I saw her lips moving as her eyebrows jumped under her eye mask. I saw that damned chin hair still, some soft lines on her throat; her

long neck, her strong round shoulder knob, the line down
to her hollow waist, the bump up over her hip that's so un-
believably beautiful it proves God's a perverted ass freak. I
kissed her bare white inner forearm again and again, I
heard the click of my lips against her skin. Loving anybody
is different from impaling anybody or getting something to
own and have. It's like trying to hug your favorite painting,
or talk to or waltz with the perfect time of day, the memory
of the most beautiful tree you ever saw.

I SLEPT HARD and woke up in such blackness. I didn't
know where I was; a hotel room is like the bottom of a well.
The air conditioner had come on during the night and the
air felt parched and dead. I tripped on the suitcase, pissed
dizzily, stood on the carpet behind the drape looking out
the window at a silver ocean and a steel-colored beach,
coal-colored sky. I lay back down, wide awake. For the next
hour or two I had the sudden profound feeling of remem-
bering Bob, out of nowhere, completely. This random on-
slaught of memories: Bob in his bathrobe, imitating Queen
Elizabeth; moving through the supermarket, spent, in slow
motion, his enormous hard-soled shoes slapping the shiny
floor; a lame nothing good-bye when I volunteered to drive
him to the airport for a six-month trip down south; the sight
of his retarded handwriting on a scrap in the kitchen we
shared. Ironing his pants in the morning, trying to get the
crotch flat. He went through an entire can of spray starch

just to make me laugh. I started laughing to myself there again, years after the fact, amazed at how Phylida could sleep and at the same time sigh so loudly there beside me.

IT WAS LIGHT out. Phylida was shoving the bed, talking.

"Did you know Ally Sheedy has a house on this island?" The doors had been thrown open and the room was filling with ocean air, the lace canopy thing above me blowing, lit with sunshine. All the humidity that had been in the air yesterday was gone. You could feel the lightness of the air. I looked out the window and saw clear to the horizon. Phylida kept talking. She'd walked around the town. She bought this hat. She just ate breakfast, and charged it to the room. She had square sunglasses under the hat on her small square nose, soft fat morning lips. Her thighs were firm, smooth vanilla hanging out of the untied white bathrobe. Underneath the robe she had her blue-flowered stretchy bikini. I saw her belly button, the giant freckle on her hip.

She took off the sunglasses to reveal two bloodshot eyes, maroon bags beneath them that reminded me of nothing so much as testicles, and said, "I don't think I slept last night."

The beginning of the end.

"I kept thinking someone was going to come into the room and kill us."

Phylida was falling apart. She was one rotation away from a seventy-two-hour-long crying jag. When these cy-

cles ended we were both a mess, and she was always a little more nuts, a little less reachable, than when they began.

"I kept hearing people on the beach."

"You thought they wanted to kill you?"

"I thought they wanted to kill you for that speech you made last night." She was about to cry. "I'm scared I'll never be able to sleep again."

"You will." I loved her, even more when she was going crazy. Now what? We had big problems. I, on the one hand, couldn't live on a wage from a bankrupt think tank. She, on the other hand, had messed her sleep rhythm up irrevocably. A surgical resident who can't sleep on command won't make it.

She said, "Are you mad at me because of last night?"

"I didn't say a thing."

"Because I didn't let you screw me?"

"Phylida, what good is any of it?"

I looked at the clock. I said I had to be at the country club two hours before her, for photos for the wedding party.

She said, "I just think we should have separate beds at home so we can sleep."

"Do what?"

Phylida shoved a towel from the bathroom into her knapsack. "Your ugly girlfriend was down there at breakfast. She asked about you." I sat up. She meant Anne, and then I remembered talking to her at dinner as she wondered if she could get more dirt from me on Bob.

"The only reason she talked to me was because I know Bob."

"Come get me on the beach before you leave. I don't want to fry."

I'M RUNNING TOWARD the bathroom, tripping out of my underwear, smelling my armpits. I put on shorts and am down at the restaurant in forty seconds. A gray wooden porch overlooking a field leading down to a marsh. Anne sat alone, drinking juice. Her coffee looked cold and bitter. She had very thin arms that she raised up, hostagelike, because I was standing above her in the sun. Her voice was all gravelly. She kept clearing her throat. "You have the nerve to show your face in public after last night?" She laughed. Yuk yuk. I acted surprised that she recognized me. She did have an abrupt set of gaping nostrils that were a little hard to look at. "Did you get all the information you needed?"

"Oh." She laughed and gestured at the other chair. "I didn't come here for that." Anyway, she said, Bob had a superb network of friends, and they'd all been saying wonderful things. She waved her hand as though, there beside her, was the network: twenty-five-year-old World Bank vice presidents, *New York Times* bureau chiefs, hedge-fund stock pickers, rich fucks who had been campaigning since they were five years old and got everything on a silver platter, lived in unbelievable apartments with wide door-ways and African carpets, and took turns powdering each other's bungholes. She said he was up for a job that was

tremendously important for the Democratic party. "We're in a formula-one race. We've got to keep the distance between us and the guy behind us." She spoke as if she were reading the directions off a box of cake mix. She said Bob could make the difference. "He's brilliant."

"Keep saying that and it'll come true."

"You're obsessed with him."

I thought back to when Bob worked at INS, Immigration and Naturalization, at Justice, how he had whole families, Rwandans who were here seeking asylum, removed from the homes where relief agencies had put them, shipped back to Africa for sure death. I asked if she knew why the U.S. stood by and watched the Hutus slaughter a million defenseless women and children with machetes.

She asked what I had against him. I said, nothing. She asked what I did for a living. "I'm a midlevel analyst at a nongovernmental research institute whose aim is to demilitarize the Western conglomerates." When I told her where, she'd never heard of it. "It's nothing. We're not important." She nodded.

I said, "When does a person stop doing what they're doing because they believe in it, and start doing it for some other cockamamie reason?"

She said, "I think it happens when you turn thirty."

It was a sunny day, Bob's special day. A breeze flicked across the tables, boats sailed silently by. I said whatever came to my head. I told her Bob and I used to work at the Boys Club on weekends, volunteering; he quit doing that.

He spent his free weekends collecting antique garbage, statues, fake Louis XIV chairs, that's why he carried all that debt on his credit cards. She nodded slowly. The last time I ran into him downtown, he stood looking at me—a pin glowed on his lapel I'd never seen before. He put out his hand but couldn't come up with my name for his friends. What a piece of shit. Why did I remember everything about him? The look on his face walking past me, at his uncle's funeral; the way he jogged, chest high, when he first got fat; the smell of the apartment he moved into with Niloo, when nothing inside it belonged to him—the couches, the fringed ottoman—and he didn't care, he didn't feel guilty, and didn't treat any of it with respect. Everything seemed to belong to Bob. Everything seemed like a joke. Anne began looking in her purse. She didn't care about what I remembered about Bob.

She said, "I once sat in the Democratic National Committee headquarters and watched Bob raise a quarter of a million dollars in forty-five minutes. He had people calling back from airplanes, from the golf course, from Australia—$10,000, $25,000, $40,000. Whatever he asked." She was glowing, her hair had come down and swept around her face suddenly and she shook her head and her nostrils filled. "It was beautiful," she said. I said nothing.

"Can you think of any possible way he'd embarrass the vice president? Drinking and driving? Smoking marijuana?" She was absolutely serious. I said no. This *was*

serious—I couldn't think of any other word for it—it was soul murder. "Soul murder," I said, half audible. She blinked for a second. "Has he ever said anything derogatory or off-color about the president or Mrs. Clinton, or the vice president or Mrs. Gore?"

"He thinks Tipper's got a fat ass."

"He's very loyal."

"Don't ask me."

"You could learn a few things about loyalty from him."

"I'm sure."

"If he's bulimic—most bulimic people I know are thin."

"Yeah, well."

"The FBI did a background check. His credit-card debt is all paid off."

Anne got up. It was a quarter to eleven. I ordered a beer. It was his wedding day, after all. I had to be at the country club at eleven-thirty. I drank it in one gulp and ordered another and barely touched it. I didn't see her again till later. I sat there for a minute and thought.

DAN, THE RICH guy, came toward me. I thought he wanted to shake hands. He simply pointed. "I can't believe you're here." Eyes narrowing, he moved away. Like many of the men in the wedding party, he wore a tuxedo that was a kind of custom job. Everyone else ignored me. We were waiting. Bob stood in his asinine four-button European tux with his hair greased back, shredding the lid of a coffee

cup with his teeth. Niles and Wayne were staying in a rented house on the other side of the island, and they were late.

"Why do all my friends hate me?" Bob said. This was a last vestige of his powerful charm, these moments of lucidity. "And people say I'm selfish."

They arrived and we pinned our flowers on and pictures were taken as we cooked in the sun in our tuxes. I overheard Bob saying that the senator was here and Madeleine Albright had arrived last night with Justice Ginsburg and that certain parts of the lawn would be secured for a landing area by Secret Service in case the weather held. But the predicted weather—terrible fog by three o'clock, scaled back from rain—would make a helicopter visit impossible. Bob sounded relieved—he was selling us on the fog, embracing the weather so something larger than himself could take the fall. "It comes in off the ocean, it looks just like smoke." Later he stood in the kitchen while I drank some ice water. "The island is transformed," he told Niles, who nodded stupidly. "All you hear is the foghorn blowing."

Bob left to change his sweat-stained shirt. Niloo told me he'd been up since five, calling everybody he knew connected to Gore. "I told him he'd better relax and forget about this business or he'd miss his whole day. He'd miss everything for what?" Her eyebrows bore down heavily and crossed. She had beautiful cinnamon-colored skin. Her eye shadow was bluish silver, and her mouth was dark cranberry red. "He just gets nuts!" I could see her thinking;

the years lay before her and she saw the loneliness and wasted effort in a flash and erased it all, and I saw her chest fall. She looked worried. I said, "I'm sure he knows you're right." Maybe I was seeing things, but there appeared to be a tiny pink mark in the center of her forehead, a flushed circle of irritated skin, with a crescent-shaped indentation inside it. Her mother came up and asked if she was ready, and they looked at each other, all perturbed. "Well," Niloo said. It might've been a scar from before.

The grounds of the country club were on a promontory, many acres jutting out into the water, with immense visibility of the western half of the island. It was a clear, crisp day. As people began to arrive you could see Bob looking up and down the coast.

Phylida was walking funny in that long dress. I could see from this distance how red she was, sunburned. "I fell asleep on the beach," she said. I had forgotten to come back to get her. Up close her face held patches of rouge. She said, "I wish I was dead." I started to apologize. She said, "This isn't your fault." She didn't actually remember applying sunblock. She said, "It hurts to have these clothes on." She was in bad shape. I asked if she wanted to have a seat. She said, "I can't bend." I asked how she got here. She made a motion to indicate she'd been lying down in the taxi. "I hate myself so much."

I said, "It's O.K." We backed into the shade and stood there, and she looked at me and whispered something. There were tears in her eyes.

"I can't believe I did this," she said. I wanted to hold her. "I'm responsible," I said. "I'll never leave you again." I told her I loved her, and I kissed the ends of her fingers because I didn't want to harm her burns. I ignored people who wanted to be seated, I let the other guys do it, and then we watched the ceremony standing. We couldn't hear any of it because the wind was blowing. She switched her weight from one foot to the other. Even her ankle was white skin striped with bright red. Afterward waiters came through with hors d'oeuvres and champagne. "Should I drink?" she said. When she'd arrived her face was flushed. Now it was pale and sweaty.

A helicopter, just a speck at first, came chopping along toward us—you could barely hear it over the surf until it was upon us. I guess the trained eye could tell from way off, this was not the vice president's official green-and-white airship. Then it hovered, knocking in the air above us, and Bob stood staring up, standing by his mom and dad, sun blazing in his copper-bristled hair.

"Paparazzi?" he said.

No. It was just some guy having a closer look at our festivities before flying away.

Phylida didn't last much longer. She asked me to take her back to the hotel. We stopped at a pharmacy and she loaded up on drugs and popped them, got some cortisone lotion, and I helped her out of those clothes and under some cool wet towels. Sometime between spreading the lo-

tion all over her body and taking off all my clothes and trying to lie on top of her, I was overcome by her frail beauty, and my mind raced through her troubled world, anything I could think of to help restore her: I said, "I'll move the bed for you, I'll find black shades, I'll buy that sound machine that mimics the rhythm of a mother's heart." I tried to think of a way she wouldn't be disturbed when I got dressed in the morning. She said, "Thank you. You're sweet."

I kissed every part of her. I realized that she was exactly what I wanted in a woman: sparkling eyes, springy hindquarters, the ability to save her own life. I felt for her then what I feel now, and knew without thinking anymore that we'd made it. Her nude hip, the most elegant line on earth, was staring me in the face. I touched her unburned parts and she smiled. We struggled to find a way I could hold her, and then suddenly it seemed we both were breathing harder.

I was unclothed and her skin burned against my unclothed body. She turned onto her stomach—I was above her, as careful as I could be—we found this to be the only angle. With her burns and loveliness and all, she pulled me in. I felt like a giant fishhook and I had her on the line and we were both rocking. I was like the Fonz with my dick right then. I tried not to touch anything except her peachy, scrumptious pillowy ass, but we were grinding and eventually I knew I was rubbing against the burned spots. She'd gotten ridden down into the bedspread and it must've felt

like sandpaper against her burns but she said nothing, making sweet painful noises and laying low and going with it; she fought me while yielding.

Afterward we ate the apples we'd brought for the plane. We found a movie on TV about a princess riding a motorcycle. As the afternoon passed I knew then that I was missing this great event, with no way of predicting who might've flown in by now. Bibi Netanyahu? Marlon Brando riding a llama? I didn't feel like I should be at one place or the other. It didn't feel like a lateral move. It felt good. We ordered crab sandwiches from town and had them delivered to the room. Sebastian returned with cake on a platter. We had a party.

EUROPEAN WEDDING

THE CONSTRUCTION SITE was walled off from the street by a makeshift bay door that Rich had padlocked from the inside. They were both flush-faced from the thought of him cheating on his fiancée, Gynnie. They stood inside the empty half-built clothing store on a busy downtown street. It was seven o'clock at night.

Their summer of flirting led them here. It felt nice to be standing beside Nora, explaining the benefits of an auxiliary water pump.

No one ever really cared about an auxiliary water pump.

The summer was over. He was about to get married. He felt protected from his life's unpleasant nauseating impending upheaval the more he joked with her and lied and led her on. It was a relief from the pussified wedding-planning crap that had taken over his brain—from the

flowery mailings, the drilling and reenameling of his teeth. Nora was the reward for getting a facial that left him bleeding and humiliated. Why was getting married so humiliating? He didn't know, but it was.

The only time she tipped her hand even slightly, a week earlier on the phone, it shook him up: "If you're so into marrying her, then why do you call me every night?"

Rich worked so closely with incoming tenants that when it came time to hand them the keys, he drove away from the site immediately, speechless, and went somewhere alone, exhausted and used up, feeling bleary. No one ever stayed in touch. The magic was in the building. Already Rich and Nora had been through a $29,000 roof-cost overrun, a sinkhole in the street. They'd taken long drives out to the country to look at celery-colored marble.

She was "sweet," and she "adored" him. She had the demeanor of a cooking-show hostess about to apologize for burning the turkey. She wore a brown cashmere cardigan, a short skirt, white knee-high socks. She sold clothes that looked like that. All over this city, preppy but sexy was in, and now she was renovating the store from scratch.

For all their long talks, he didn't know much about her. She was violently allergic to nuts, she played soccer in college. He didn't know, for instance, her age, what decade she played soccer in college. She had thick, creamy makeup, a face that quickly shifted to record any injury. Her walk was jumbled, stilted, uneven but purposeful; it im-

plied a hip injury from childhood that came back and plagued her when it rained. She had a dozen decisions to make tonight about the street-level floor plan so walls could go up next week, questions from the engineers about louvered mezzanine windows, questions about plumbing from the project superintendent.

Nora was his only client. Nora's happiness was his full-time job.

"You like working with me because I'm lovable—because you love me," she said once, hoarse from a cold, her voice breaking, hacking in fits.

She had a weirdly shaped head, long in the back, which haunted him. He'd tried to add her strangeness to that well of all women's mysteries.

She had a long, slightly crooked nose, really good perfume. The fact that she wasn't Gynnie, the wrongness of it—she existed apart from the feminine regime that disoriented him. She was someone else. She could die tomorrow, he didn't care.

There was nobody in the building but them, and they'd been talking about the structural column that would go where they stood to support a staircase that wasn't in yet. Nora stomped on his foot. He pushed her. She laughed. They went from that to, like, silence. He was looking at her big lips, so nervous he had flulike symptoms. He knew it was there for the taking. God, he deserved a little makeout session.

There'd been some months of lead-up to this moment, and their bodies came together and their arms went around each other with such excitement and relief that a sobbing noise or a grunt got stuck in her throat. He measured her in terms of his fiancée—he thought she was a few multiples in width. Nora fell into the category of women who are not fat, whose hair is bigger, who know how to dress themselves with wide belts, nail polish, jewelry. The kiss was quick, she tasted like cosmetic powder, he felt relieved and wanted to finish the walk-through and get out of there. He felt a pressure from her mouth, broad and forceful, her tongue pressing forward, and he tried to meet her tongue but it pushed his out of the way and came deeper into his mouth. In the very delicate balance between what is sexy or risky, her tongue was difficult to make room for.

He stood back, tried to smile, to breathe, to change the rhythm of the tongue thing she just did. She had a curious look on her face, one of vacancy and desire.

She moved closer, opening her mouth wide; tiny white strings of opaque spit had formed, like webs, in the corners of her mouth. She licked her lower lip, which had become dry and pitted. Some of her lipstick had come off. She grabbed the back of his head and jacked it toward her. Her own head moved forward steadily—like a shark's head, like a prosthetic limb, some football wrapped in bologna. She threw her tongue down his throat like a waterlogged sneaker.

He maintained his footing, jaw open, impaled.

She leaned back and said things like, "OOHHH fuck!" and "Finally."

Kissing her was so terrible he stopped and thought of what to do next.

This was his only client, and if he offended her or did something ugly—she owned the building.

You idiot, idiot, idiot.

This was supposed to be some dreamy diversion, but it was turning out not so good.

He didn't know what else to do, so he tried her bon-bons. She took off her cardigan, then her shirt.

Her bra was sheer, simple lace netting, with no decoration on it. She had fine stretch marks at the top of her chest. She had goose bumps on her hairless arms. There were other smells now, among the ammoniac and dusty smell of glue guns, tar sealant, Sheetrock dust. There was some smell coming off her, her smell—he thought of chick-peas and deodorant. Most of the gutted first floor was dark behind her, and she backed up. Looking directly at him, she undid her skirt, which opened like a kilt, and dropped it. She came forward in the loafers and knee socks and underwear. She seemed huge now, making goo-goo eyes. She was the biggest girl who'd ever made goo-goo eyes at him. She reached out and pulled on his nuts, which hurt.

He took off her bra. Her tits—fell *down*. He tried to raise one up to normal height, where it had been in the bra,

and then he tried the other. *Bloop.* Like deflated bags of water, hanging to the waistband of her undies, cold, the consistency of chunky soup. She looked at him, her sad eyes smiling, her sad mouth looking for its tongue, her sad tongue looking for a crack in her lower lip to lick.

What *was* this?

She asked him if he was nervous. He wasn't nervous.

She examined and squeezed his behind. His hand slid across her stomach and felt soft, pillowy fat. And then she stepped back and lifted one leg and then the other, humming quietly, and he realized she was dancing.

She owned the one and only building he was building. Her father owned the other project Rich's company was in the process of constructing, a $125 million deal about a mile from here involving forty subcontractors from around the country—a job so huge Rich had been relegated to underground utilities and landscaping. He wasn't in any position to push her away. He could feel the vast inexperience of a woman of complete fragility, shielded by her wealth, with a lot of power, reacting to his withdrawal.

"I'm getting married in three days and you are disgusting" was what he wanted to say. "Haven't you ever just goofed around a little? Why don't you put your clothes back on?"

He had to get out of here because he had to be at the airport by eleven tonight so he could fly to France to get married on Saturday.

"My darling," she said to him, and pulled his head to her chest.

A LITTLE LATER, he was caught in a kind of eternal now—an eternally present moment—adrift, but where? They were on the floor, she was mostly on the concrete, he was mostly in the dirt, trying to breathe through the top of his head.

How long could this go on? Had she ever orgasmed in her life?

The giblets were only palatable if you were horny and liked the person, he now had learned.

What was happening to him was, he observed, actually worse than any punishment he was going to get from Gynnie, if he told her, which he would; he'd have to. He saw now that there would be no good way to do it. He felt as if he'd been singled out for some kind of crystalline moral instruction. He tried to zone out; he pictured lying on a beach in Rio, reading a magazine, eating the same ripe plum over and over. He looked at his watch. In fifteen more minutes he would quit. He began rewriting this time of his existence into the untrue negative: "I never befriended Nora Garleck outside of work. I am not lying here now."

Am I in hell? he thought, awhile later. She rode against his nose, getting closer. She launched her pelvis many inches into the air, and then down, then up again, like an

old Greco-Roman wrestler trying to earn a fighter's wage, to keep from being pinned. Gynnie was on the beach in Rio with Rich as he ate his plum again and again, and she looked gorgeous in her bikini—as always, an epiphany. Rich actually began to picture Gynnie helping him escape: She urged him to finish eating the plum so they could go swim—it didn't make any sense, but he thought of her beside him in those moments, and it did save him. Of course, in reality, she didn't know where he was, and if and when she did find out she would dump him and never speak to or look at him ever again.

"ARRRGHH!" Nora yelled. What made her yelling so awful was not any fear that a passing stroller might hear her or come onto the site—though during the last few moments Rich had begun hoping that a crazy person would break in and beat them to death with the spade beside Nora's writhing head. What made her yelling awful was the sound—a lonely yell, from a woman who didn't have boyfriends, who would have to be satisfied with this degraded scene for months, who didn't have to worry about what Rich thought of her, because she knew he wouldn't be calling ever again except with a catastrophic problem about the renovation. At the end she crammed his head into her with the fearsome power of a combat-ready United States Marine feeding on adrenaline, her body like a vise, yelled, "RRAAGGHH," like a butcher in a poker game, like a buckshot gorilla, and he felt like crying. He could've thrown up at any time, lying there in the dirt; and to think

he'd done this in the name of love, in the name of freedom, of a last fling.

RICH WAS SO happy to be home he felt like hugging his porch, like squeezing the bag of rotten leaves like a pony, tossing the leaves in the air; like grabbing his neighbor—as the man silently loaded bottles into his recycling bin, with his back to Rich—and kissing the man. Rich stood, his face abraded from shaved crotch whiskers; he wanted to say hello, make small talk, tell the man what had happened tonight, but he would've fallen apart. That long-headed freaky spit factory would be stalking Rich when he got back from his honeymoon, he was now sure of it.

The UPS man had left a box wedged between the storm door and the front door. He kicked it in with the mail. He could hear the packing pellets shaking inside it. Untouched mail from the last five days lay on the floor. A few last response cards. He knew the answer by this late date. This European wedding idea had stunned a lot of people who didn't feel like spending two thousand dollars on a trip to fucking France. He understood that finally and wasn't mad. He read each card, carefully appreciating whatever little apology they made, even one with only the "Will not attend" box checked off.

Standing in the little living room, Rich was suddenly grateful for everything in his life. He'd been living the last months as a prologue to rather than a passing through of life's events, and as he stared at the suitcases, he realized

that now he had begun to "care" again. The last months had felt like a gap, an era of holding breath. He'd been vehemently ignoring with his whole heart whatever happened to him each day, but now it did, finally, make sense, and he was glad for however it was that the obfuscation of his brain had ended. In an attempt to distract himself he'd spent a million hours on the phone with Nora every night, ostensibly for work, and when she didn't answer he poured over blueprints, and when he could see every angle in three dimensions with his eyes closed he tried reading *A Tale of Two Cities*. He never got past that first loony sentence and ditched the book, but now it, too, finally, made sense. This *was* the best of times, *and* the worst of times.

Like tonight, for instance. He ate Nora's pussy, and now, for the first time since April (it was August), he was glad to be home. See?

Like his home—a haven, technically, which he'd worked so hard to make cozy and familiar, a place to relax, to fall apart, to heal. Six months ago he stopped coming here except to sleep and eat, because it was Gynnie's terrain to unload her misery upon him—"I can't get the coffee filters apart, I can't cope"—never acting like her old self, from six o'clock in the morning on. See? Contradiction.

Outside the house, it was a fun time of getting engaged, of wearing a tuxedo at a fancy engagement party thrown in their honor, of being so proud of Gynnie while everyone tripped over one another in tuxes and long dresses, trying

to be charming; lazily wondering to himself about their future, enjoying the subtle closeness as the lines fuzzed between someone you have sex with and someone you need beside you, everywhere, to make it real. And after the first twenty minutes at the party he stopped talking to her, because he wanted to kick back (because she couldn't handle herself in front of people, because she could sound like an idiot if you listened too closely), *because he felt like it,* and he drank and smoked cigarettes and pot, he kept moving, walking out of a room when she walked in, mocking her in front of her own boss for repeating his name. He'd done all he could to get the party to loosen up, but it didn't work, and in the car on the way home she screamed and swung at him—*scratching his cornea!*—he pulled the car over, she lifted her springy, catlike appendage and came so close to kicking him that he'd already accepted it, whatever bones broke, whatever changes came from the fact that she had kicked him in the head while driving drunk while they were engaged, and then he grabbed her foot and they almost had a fistfight in the car. She was a small person and he'd hoped to bully her but that hadn't worked out.

They were in a potentially terrible place.

Why did he do that?

He spent the rest of the summer preejaculating, scared. It seemed like a proximity issue.

It was evenings of eating under trees in the park out of Tupperware by a pond in the sunset, weekends in front of

the fireplace, the house filling with smoky wood smell, of thinking to himself, This is a decent chance for the love that everyone wants in their life. A time of trying to learn to *like* her, to be gentle and nice, because that worked with girls. It was a time of newfound humility.

Everything was changing so fast. He tried to keep some distance between them to slow it down. Which was like trying to slow down a bullet with a chocolate-chip cookie.

Rich was trying to know her, but of course he couldn't know her, because now he was marrying her, because he *was* her now and you can't understand what you are while you're in it. She had been miserable since they got engaged, and had let him know it. It wasn't her fault, he understood, because he, too, was now turning into a short lady with skirts and buckled shoes, a hundred and eleven pounds, trying to keep it under control. A number of things led to her/their misery, and all were his fault. The skin under her armpits broke out from his cheap CVS lotion; her right hip was sore from screwing, her leg became shorter, her left knee and ankle went wrong from that—see how he'd torn her apart by this engagement? By his stabbing her with his penis he'd sprained a muscle on her hip that was *too delicate for engagement*. Her shoes, the best ones, were now defunct. She would come down in the morning and hold a toe out toward his cereal—"See how my flats are awful?" She could no longer go to the gym, she could no longer do African dance, she could no longer eat turkey sausages because they gave her gas. "Boys eat that

stuff." He burnt his sausages in a frying pan, and the burnt parts could give a person cancer, but the fumes made her hungry so she ate. In the spring, she began her protest. If he cooked meats, she ate shaves of green salad off the tip of a razor-sharp cleaver, with lemon; she threw away her fruit half eaten, stood over the garbage and yawned and it fell out.

He opened up a gift from Gynnie's aunt in Europe and out came a broken antique cuckoo clock.

She dropped so much weight her ass wrinkled. He shared her pain. They were both cramping, aging, walking stiffly. He slept in a push-up position. He was sort of atrophying, moving as if his feet had been burned, in a shortened stride, like Dr. Locascio, his dental surgeon, who he hated. She was walking like Barney the purple dinosaur, empty smile, her hands clasped in front of her. They'd reached this state of disrepair from holding it together.

Gynnie had left a message (she was already in France—it was evening here, it was very late there). He called Martina's house, where the event would take place, and somehow Gynnie picked up the phone. He was so glad to hear her sweet whispering voice that he felt like crying and silently prayed to love her forever. He thought she might have said, "I love you so much," and was already delivered to her, kind of swooning, and asked her to repeat herself because the connection was weird and he wanted to hear those words again.

She said, "If my tiara gets bent I'm going to kill myself."

He said he'd packed it in a shoe box.

She said, "Emile Marcus sent us a check for five thousand dollars."

He said, "Who?"

She said, "An old friend of my mom's."

She said that Rich's mother and some of the other women in his family had arrived there safely, and she, Gynnie, was now feeling upset. Rich had a big family, and in his mind it seemed like the arrival of the women was what got you upset. Rich's mom, her sisters—his four aunts between forty and sixty—many girl cousins who he'd grown up with, played tag and footsie with and watched develop, his two beautiful younger sisters, who he loved, were all already in France. They were a close group and had fallen for the romantic idea of a trip to France as soon as Rich let his mother in on the wedding plan, and began planning their own trip to coincide. The e-mails of the women in his family were filled with endless logistics, ways to dodge frequent-flyer blackouts, how to wear the same outfit over and over, what kind of underpants you could buy in Paris that they didn't sell in Saks. Fights about who would share a hotel room; fights about how beautiful Rich was as a baby, more beautiful than a girl; anatomical descriptions of hysterectomies; the pets—"If she brings Selma, I bring Fluffy." They were children, looking for trouble. When he couldn't take it anymore, he simply put them in touch with Martina, online, and Martina's Italian, French, Swiss, German, and Spanish aunts, cousins, and nieces joined in,

offering ideas to their future in-laws from the States, all using third-grade English so everyone could understand, so that the e-mail traffic became a wonderful if somewhat cryptic source of winery-stinky-cheese-château-barge-tour-lakeside-yoga-nostril-breathing-retreat suggestions. (During World War II, Gynnie's mom's family got bombed out of her hometown, a little city near Strasbourg, and when the war ended they spread like airborne diaspora. They hated France and Germany, where they were from. They became antinationalist, anticapitalist missionaries. They became shrinks and painters, trying to make peace. There were no men, for some reason, breathing, in that group. The men of Gynnie's family were all in the ground.) Very quickly the globe was knit in the plans surrounding their wedding, forming a bond encasing the bridal couple. He didn't want any more phone calls on satellite time delay from some old frau in broken cuckoo-clock land. They were already interfering with his ability to see Gynnie—they were guaranteed to be in the way when he got married. Before Rich even saw the French château Martina had been rebuilding by hand, alone, with her dead husband's money—before he stepped across her front yard of Roman ruins in the little Loire valley town of Cravat—eighteen girls and women, soon-to-be in-laws who had dusted off their high school accents across seven languages, were falling in love in their nightgowns. Rich could hear his mother in the background, trying to clear her throat, the excitement in her rising voice. That night, Gyn-

nie had taken a boat ride down the "Lo-arr"—that was how his mother pronounced it—and they were all still dizzy. They'd reveled as they motored into the sunset about what a colossal mistake the men had made by not coming until Friday. Rich would take the last flight out tonight, Wednesday, arrive Thursday at noon. His brother and father and best man had let Rich know ("Faggoty, Euro bullshit") that the less time they spent in France the better. None of them knew French. They weren't interested. He didn't know French either, but he wasn't afraid. They were afraid, and did what men in Rich's family did when they didn't like the odds against them: made fun of it and gave up. They'd be there with his uncles, Howard and Shel, and his cousins, Seth, Daniel, and Charles, by dinnertime on Friday.

"Your family," Gynnie said. "Your mother."

"Is everyone having a nice time?" A pause in communication, a weird gap of overseas static. He waited for something else.

Gynnie wondered if Rich really wanted to know. She could see everything, exposed, as though for the first time, a system functioning with all of its absurdities. Not so much like "the elephant in the room that no one wants to talk about," as she'd said in the past, in the middle of a less threatening crisis, but like a planet, turning, with all its immense, fantastic permanence and emanation. No wonder you're still so fucked up, she thought, and then just said it, "No wonder you're still so fucked up," and felt much better.

"What do you mean?"

"Why do you call her Mommy? What's with everybody sitting on everybody's lap? What's with everybody going to the bathroom in pairs?"

"We don't want the other people to be lonely."

"They talk about farts. They talk about house pets."

"Yeah?"

"They smoke."

He didn't say anything. She giggled uncomfortably. "Your mother wants to say hello."

Rich's mother reminded him to pack the expensive hairbrush she'd sent him in the little purple velvet bag with the silver drawstring and his initials monogrammed on it. He didn't see what the problem was in this innocent conversation, or in anything else she'd ever done. His mother had bent over backward for him all his life. In fact, he'd thrown the brush away when he got it—he didn't use a hairbrush, and the sight of it, of its daintiness, made him feel like he was being asphyxiated. He said he would go find the brush as soon as he hung up. He was dying to tell his mother about the nightmare with Nora but didn't know how. There wasn't time. His mother was not his confidante anymore.

EARLY THAT NEXT morning, in a farming town in the shadow of a nuclear reactor in the southern part of France, Emile Marcus tried to buy a sandwich for the long ride to the wedding in Cravat. He'd had a small piece of his throat and some of the tissue in his sinuses removed, along with a

part of his upper lip—not much—and the scar that ran from his right nostril down to his collarbone had healed months earlier, but still, sometimes, he felt it impeded his speech so that he wasn't being clearly understood. He spoke to a mustached teenage boy behind the case with the face of a cartoon baby; the boy winced sullenly. As Emile repeated himself, two young women asked for the very same sandwiches and were served. He spoke a third time; another patron appeared to his left. Emile was staring at the cutting board covered with lettuce, brie, sliced hard-boiled egg. Is this a joke? he asked himself.

He saw himself at the age of this idiot behind the sand-wich case, peddling scavenged broken chair rungs and pieces of timber for firewood in a town that had been bombed back to the Stone Age—he stood straight, built himself from the soles of his flat feet, remembered how badly he'd hoped to escape Europe after the war, the complete obliteration of agriculture—sewage disposal—that next fifteen years, a time of particular misery for people with German blood, took his hands out of his pock-ets, dropped his voice, and spoke one last time, slowly, steadily, raving, leaning into it, scaring the kid. He got the sandwich.

He went into the post office to check his mail. He knew how to walk into a place and make people turn and look. Everything about his demeanor said that he had reached a certain level of success, he had a certain bearing still.

He had swept-back hair, a corduroy shirt, varicose veins

on his legs, linen shorts, purple feet; he had the tall, broad-shouldered bearing of an airline pilot, a 1950s bus driver. He wore aviator sunglasses, donned them as he came back out into the haze. He drove a car that smelled like sweat—he got a sweaty back from driving it. It had a wooden steering wheel—it was cracked and yellow and splintering, like his teeth. He felt like royalty in this car, not so much in its present shape but originally, left over from way back when. He had the collar of his corduroy shirt turned up; he wore a fine piece of fisherman's netting, dyed black, as a scarf. He didn't know where he'd got it—did it belong to his thirty-seven-year-old girlfriend, Ariel? It looked like snot. It looked like that steel-wool junk coming out of mussels. He thought it gave him panache. He had pink zits on his hands from the chemicals in the swimming pool at the apartment complex.

He had a nasty letter from Ariel in his pocket; he had no room for her in his heart, or for her four-year-old, thirty-five pound daughter, Lydia—there was nothing to do now but try to force them out of the house, get the city to turn off the heat and electricity and wait until winter.

He'd secured a box at the post office because at the temporary apartment he'd taken—until he could sort things out and go home—they threw his mail on the floor in the foyer with everyone else's. Parked beside the post office, with the top down, the car rumbled softly, like a speedboat in neutral. He had some clothes in a train case, the sandwich, two cameras in a small silver valise in the backseat; in

the coming days, if he became too disgusted with himself, he could go off, try to photograph something beautiful, a portrait worth money that he would gladly give away to his American "niece," Gynnie. For some reason, this last round of misery with Ariel had begun with the announcement of the wedding event. The news had simply driven him nuts—with jealousy? Not exactly. He tried to shake it off. He absolutely would not be able to miss this, but wanted to know why he cared so much. Yet at the same time he was dreading the loneliness of a weekend with strangers so badly he'd bought a book of crossword puzzles so he wouldn't have to look up if anyone spoke. His meanness and discomfort around Ariel had to do with Gynnie, maybe. Ever since Gynnie's mother, Martina, called him, he'd been toting up his life, with the excuse that he was trying to calculate how much he could afford to send as a wedding gift, but each time he reached the end of the tally, he found himself in the basement handling his old rifle, thinking about shooting himself, wondering if it worked. But why? He had nothing like a family anywhere else; Gynnie was a good girl, she'd always been in his heart despite the miles between them, he'd saved the sweet, empty letters she'd sent over years, he showered her with dresses and jewelry he'd picked up on photo shoots, brought them to her in garbage bags on his sporadic visits across the decades; Martina kept him updated on her struggles. He thought of her always with a smile.

Also, she was quite possibly the product of his own testicles.

He realized that if he ate here at the wheel he would get crumbs on his pants. His mind oscillated like this for a while.

The car's idle was still a little bit rough.

He had a real affinity for repulsive American overkill: He'd sent that check to Gynnie—this was money he needed to live—partly out of guilt, partly out of longing to be included, partly hoping she'd use the money to push the ceremony over the edge into a freak show spectacle of empty American pomposity, ruin it. He had a black suit for the event. He didn't remember when it had begun looking wrong—the top and bottom were two different blacks. After forty years as a photographer he knew colors of clothing, but somehow he'd lost track, coming and going from that little dump above a darkroom he slept in on his visits to Paris, now that he no longer had his own place there. He decided to eat the sandwich while parked on the street. He thought that his whole life had been a waste, an internal, hidden, lonely solitude, rather than the glorious escape he'd planned as a boy (to what?). He felt bitter in a way that made his face collapse and fold around his scar.

On the road leading out of town, a paper bag flew up onto Emile's windshield, wedged itself under the windshield wiper, and stayed. He drove like that for the next four hours, pushing the engine, thinking of what he would

say to Martina about Ariel and her little poker-faced kid not being with him.

AS EMILE DROVE toward Cravat, Rich woke up, after napping an hour. Then he drove to the airport. Inside the terminal, he was so uptight he almost punched the ticketing agent for telling him the weather overseas. The plane took off, the city unrolled beneath him, and he went through his thinking: I did not lie on the floor with her, did not rub saliva on her snatch, did not promise a lot more where that came from. In twenty minutes the plane leveled.

Beneath him, a hurricane twice the length of Florida moved toward the East Coast; it was two hundred miles off North Carolina. Four hours from now, Boston to St. Augustine would be in it. All down the East Coast, airports would be closing. By early Friday morning, furious and exhausted from sleeping at a different airport the night before, the male members of Rich's family would be arriving at an airport outside of Cleveland, among a deluge of important people with commitments overseas.

SHE LAY AWAKE, thinking. She thought of all these different odd moments in her life: The funny gymsuit they wore in fourth grade—she unzipped it to go to the bathroom and the top fell in the toilet. Sniffing glue at her friend Dina Whitticomb's Halloween party, sophomore year in high school, the night after her brother died—it took away her

sadness, she felt no fear. The mugging on 110th Street at Barnard. The morning of the TWA bombing—after an emergency meeting at Langley, she left work with an awful urinary infection and peed on the floor of a grocery store. She'd only peed a single drop. The grocery store was on P Street!

The room was egg-yolk color with fake-marble red streaks, veins, like someone had thrown up, she decided— eggs and blood. This was "Gynnie's room." Of course it wasn't her room—she had no plans to come back here ever again in her life. This "château" her mother was rebuilding would probably fall down before she could get back. Gynnie stretched and thought with some relief, in her status as a bride, about her former boyfriends, how each of their lives had improved during her tenure, and gone right downhill again after the breakup: one more reason to believe that Rich was the one—his life had not improved at all since they met. And compared to her old boyfriends . . . But look at who she was comparing him to: A guy who took stuff out of people's cars, probably in jail by now. A gay guy (also a felon—he stole stuff "for the band"). A gorgeous liar with such an overexaggerated sense of himself he still hadn't figured out that she'd dumped him. An alcoholic research chemist who could have made a lot of money. And the married guy, who as his main selling point convinced Gynnie he might leave his wife to marry her, because after all, he'd already proven he was the marrying kind! Rich *was* the marrying kind—he had finally come across. It was

among the many strange truths of their relationship: Their coming together had been fairly painless and benign. She thought that the nastiest times came about from neglect, from *not* seeing each other—simple as that. The slow destruction began every Monday morning, when they headed back to hell, and was undone again by the time the following Monday morning rolled around. By Wednesday evening she'd forgotten him. Dinnertime she picked fights. Sleep was another exhausting commitment. Sex midweek felt about as spiritual as a bowel movement.

Sometimes you just didn't feel like being in love.

And they were uncomfortable speaking about the big things that bothered them; bad communication always made her lonely. Their social life was cold, work-related. They weren't crazy about each other's friends.

Gynnie didn't know what time it was—there was no clock in here. It was typical of her mother, Gynnie thought, lying in the room of shiny egg yoke that drove her to want to knife herself—that she'd been able to trick Gynnie into marrying Rich in a house she'd never been in, in a country she didn't know anything about, her mother's "homeland." Why couldn't she get married in the perfectly nice house in Winnetka where she'd actually grown up?

She didn't know.

She never knew her mother spoke German, Swiss, and Dutch, on top of French. She didn't know her mother was descended from a count. She didn't know her mother's family owned metal-machining and ball-bearing factories

in Germany during the war. These last few days, drowning in a sea of foreign aunties with all their amazing stories had been—whatever. She didn't know her mother lived in a stable after the war, didn't know her father looked considerably older; he should've—he spent their whole marriage dying. She'd never met him. Nobody ever told her anything. The people close to her ran some covert operation designed to save her from any pain. And so she'd take their crummy advice; she never knew what was going on— in conversations, in movies, always dragging on someone's sleeve asking for a report, always walking into the middle of a silent room, mystified, trying not to get paranoid about people staring at her.

In regular life you could go off and figure things out, major things; she knew what recommendations to make to her boss at the Department of State about events developing around the globe, how to respond to Sudanese maniacs, wreaking havoc on their darker-skinned countrymen, genociding them down there, she knew that when three thousand boys turned up in the desert with kwashiorkor from eating leaves after being hunted all winter, it was time to make her case, beg for increased U.S. Naval presence off the coast of Somalia. These were things she could grasp.

But she didn't know why her mom's family left Germany, didn't know that the years after the Weimar Republic were not only years of loneliness and frustration in their new homeland in France but years of profit and silence and guilt and inaction; she couldn't get a straight answer from

her aunts about why, after the Nazi era, the Zimmers then ran out of France. She wanted to hear what they'd gone through, firsthand—know her past, see herself. Why had Martina waited until yesterday to tell Gynnie she was leaving her this house? The last count lived here in the fifteenth century. Who lived here after that? Her mother told people she'd been "communicating" with the count.

So here she was sitting in fucking France, didn't know what time it was, never got the woman on the phone who promised to do her hair Saturday—today was Thursday—barely spoke the language, and there was no one here to marry anyway.

She'd always felt this disconnection. When she was four, some other kids explained that she was one parent short. As she grew up her mother filled in the blanks with dippy anecdotes: "He always loved Sunday mornings." As a teenager she was so sweetly pretty, people brightened up automatically when she appeared. She hated that; it threw her off. As a teenager her brother got killed in the front seat of a car coming back from a Police concert. Five other people, including the driver, who'd fallen asleep, walked away from the wreck. To this day people tried talking to her about Noel. She was angry. The driver was still a "friend of the family," came to see them on Christmas. Picture something so terrible that for the rest of your life it never changes and you don't know how to deal with it.

Since his death, she'd always had one ear to another world, whatever that meant. Kept half a step toward the

grave, to be closer. She couldn't hear anything, but she was leaning that way.

For that reason she was often about as fun and easygoing as a ligament. In a way, she was already dead. But now, after a long period of hoping she would die, of having a zombielike attitude, she was a little bit surprised at herself. She felt like trying. Not so much in a sexual sense, though sex with Rich had the potential of being something more than a patient licking, an accomplished getting off, and a kind, attentive manner afterward. But it wasn't that. What stuck with Gynnie was the question this guy posed, because she liked him. If you like him, will he stay? Didn't he already hate her? Hadn't she already submitted her résumé for this task force on terrorism that would put her on the road, sleeping in hotels, two hundred nights next year?

Two days before her wedding was not the time to be in an awful mood. Rich would be here by lunch. Was she supposed to pick him up? Was it even legal for her to drive in France? The important thing was to enjoy herself. This was the mind-blowing time of getting married overseas, of a new life, of having different hair, shorter, parted on the side but really fluffed up so that it bounced more—her hair was so much better cut short. Which explained everything that had evaded her to this day—she might have been Clinton's first female deputy director of communications if she hadn't had that long, beat, flat Fiona Apple hair in the interview—her old haircut was part of her sorrow this

morning. If she'd had this new fluffy haircut, if she hadn't been so tense with her answers, and then insecure, lashing out, clamming up. A person ought to be given more than one big chance in life.

She hadn't had her period in six months. She didn't weigh enough. She wore two beepers for work, had a secure line installed in their house, to the assistant secretary of State for North Africa and the Middle East. She couldn't calm down at night, scrubbed her kitchen floor on her hands and knees with a paper towel. Rich was forced to watch—he promised that no matter what happened he would let her do this. In the morning she put the milk away in the plates cabinet—the smell of rotten milk meant she was tired. She gave herself B_{12} shots through her stockings in her thigh at her desk; she was so tired at night she hallucinated in the shadows in the parking lot that mice were running after her; her greatest fear in life was that bugs would come crawling out of her skin. One day she'd tell Rich everything.

She believed all the corny stuff about marriage, and it worked—gave her stability. It was something eternal, he was the one true love of her life, hopefully; she had given herself to him completely.

TWO HOURS SOUTH of Paris toward Borges was Cravat, a forgettable medieval village that sat up on a mound, like a painting of Tuscany, rising out of a fertile valley. Vineyards formed a patchwork, the Loire running through the broad

expanse. From the main road looking up, Rich could see, among the trees, an enormous château owned by a famous champagne family. Beside it, one small, black spire of Gynnie's mother's house jabbed up at the sky.

The road corkscrewed around the hilltop through narrow streets crowded with tourists drinking outdoors, riding by on motorbikes dressed in soccer jerseys, taking photos of the view. In Martina's yard, as he'd heard, some gray carved ruins from a Roman fountain. He didn't have time to look, though, because the girls and women who'd been in his life forever were moving toward him, grabbing and kissing him. His aunts and cousins—he had nine girl cousins, seven were here with their mothers, some looked frightened, others were better traveled, but they all seemed pretty excited. His sweet little sister Connie ran out the door toward him. He turned, eyes locked on her, arms flung open, and swung her in the air as if to say, "I have always loved you uncontrollably, we are in a strange place, you and me. Hold me." Then his other little sister, Jenny, ran out the door, and he did the same thing with her.

It *was* a romantic place; you never saw anything like this wine-country relic along the beaten tourist path—an old French château, tilting down the hill in sand-colored stucco, the wisteria climbing, a birdbath entwined in roses, a rusted scythe, an old woman staring out her second-story window across the street at them, the oaken smell of burning twigs in the vineyard fields; they were all here for some wedding-bell crap. You could see it ringing in all these

women's heads, written on their faces—it looked like they wanted to eat him.

His cousin Tina wore a black-eyed Susan in her hair, stretch Capri pants, a midriff T-shirt; his sister Connie wore a bathing suit and cutoffs; his cousin Shelley in pigtails, glasses, grinning, reached over and unfolded the collar of the shirt he'd slept in. Everyone wore lip gloss, everyone was open to him. They all seemed buzzed on the place. Beneath Connie were pretty little girls with long hair speaking something other than English, pulling at his bags. The other women smiled at their clowning. Like girls in a girls' dormitory who had begun menstruating together, the group was operating through some primal communication.

He hugged his mother. "*Mommy*. Where am I?" he wanted to say. Neither of them could speak. She seemed ashamed and excited. Staring at her, Rich suddenly remembered his dream from hours earlier on the airplane; he'd slept soundly, and not before this instant—not after waking, not while driving, preoccupied, on the road from Paris—had this wild, foggy, sweet dream from the plane come back to him, a dream of screwing his mother. "I can't believe it's you, Mom," he kept saying in the dream, but it was her, and it was impossibly good. The image of it stung him and he froze, baffled, forcing it from his mind. He asked where Gynnie was, and ten people said at once that she was napping and not to wake her.

Rich shook hands with Emile Marcus. He thanked him for the check. Emile's hand was big and warm, weathered smooth, like a baseball mitt left in the sun. Emile said something Rich couldn't understand. Rich met an old woman named Marie—"Nice to meet." After fifteen minutes of greetings, Rich's mother and his sisters moved him toward the house; his mother said she'd be wearing all black for the wedding, and wondered if that pleased him. She began describing the dress. Unlike the mess he'd left behind, there was no Nora here, no threat of any kind. He looked out across the old sloping rooftops of the town, the cobblestone streets, out onto the valley, and felt like he was in a Three Musketeers movie.

GYNNIE LAY ON the bed, propped up, reading *Shape* magazine. On her arrival in Paris she had spent time at a department store makeup counter, and since then had been doing an Asian thing with her look. Hair pulled up tightly in barrettes so her eyes narrowed like an Eskimo's, eyeliner pencil, short kimono robe.

She made no move to get up, and said hello in a whisper. Rich leaned over and hugged her. He could feel her warm body through the kimono. She might've been wearing little shorts underneath. Her toenails were painted to match the eye shadow. He noticed as he hugged her that she smelled like flowers, and that he smelled like BO. He was too tired to shower. Transition to a French person complete.

Rich unzipped his suitcase.

"That's your side of the room, those are your drawers," she said.

Rich pulled out some clothes and looked at them. "Why are we doing this?" he said.

She sighed, spent. "Why?" Did she have to answer this question for him, too, when they couldn't do anything to stop it? "Because we're desperate and we're lonely and nothing better came along." She felt small and tired and afraid. "You're all I've got now, and you'd better get used to it. We're on the grown-up train, and we don't get off until the graveyard."

Rich held up his folded shirts. He said he was talking about the clothes. As in, Why not leave them in the suitcase and forget the dresser?

Gynnie moved to a chair in the corner and opened a book on castles in France. She was able to breathe so shallowly, so infrequently, she looked like she was suspended in formaldehyde. At home, over the last six months, when she felt bad, her mind had traveled to French castles, to the French Language Institute classes she never made because of work, to the tapes she didn't listen to in the car, to the photographs of this house and yard, swatches of paint. In the hallucination she slipped sideways into the postcard-perfect photo she kept in her Filofax, met farmers who wore brown weathered berets made of beaver pelts, who told stories of Martina as a girl jumping in haystacks, never mentioned the bombing raids, gang rapes by Russian sol-

diers, Hitler's need for steel ball bearings. Now, actually being here in France, where could she imagine herself?

Rich dropped his shirts, ashamed, wanting to put his hand on Gynnie, and stood in the mirror above her and combed out his slept-on hair and said, "Now I know why they call it the red-eye."

OUT BACK RICH found his mother and Martina standing together, arms folded, contemplative. They were considering what might jazz up the ceremony, using their respective advanced degrees in the Bala Institute's Fire and Water Six-Week Breathing Course and a Ph.D. in contemporary American art. The backyard was mired in the same eternal junk heap as out front—a bent weather vane, farm machinery from the Middle Ages, a two-foot-thick table constructed from a single tree, hand-sawed—take a guess. Stone Age? Old old crap. Actual graffiti and other evidence of age-old vandalism—a Norman cross had been carved into the foundation of the house—the church had stopped using Norman crosses before the Crusades. Rich's mother stepped up to the fourteenth-century altar and described how she'd be lighting what appeared to be a small broom, made out of sage, and as it smoldered overhead, she'd be wiggling and dancing it in the air—it was a Native American tradition—in a light, swaying hula style, 1940s Camp-Hialeah-Gitchee-Goomee style, across the entire wedding party, to cleanse them psychically.

Gynnie came out with sunglasses on and sat by the wall

with her feet up on a paint can, checking her pedicure. In the sunlight Rich thought she looked like she needed a blood transfusion. From this distance she looked like Connie's twin, same head, but then she crossed her legs identically to the way Jenny did, down to the way her toes curled. It was weird. Martina asked if he wanted to walk into the ceremony led by his mother or father or both or alone.

Since he'd stepped outside he'd picked up on a distinct earthy smell that reminded him of semen.

Rich's mother walked over and said, "Do you want to eat the best cookie you ever had in your life?" She stared into his face for a long second and grabbed it and kissed him on the mouth. She said he was a "beautiful, lovely boy." Rich said, "What the heck is that smell?"

"It's the tree," his aunt Patti said. It had long green flowers that looked like peapods. He watched it shake in the breeze as people walked around the corner to the patio for lunch.

He sat beneath the tree on a long bench; it was a pew of some fine hard wood that had been left out in the rain for centuries. Everything in the yard was like this: old, alive, in use, together. Time didn't pass in this town. He sat wondering, as he heard his mother and aunts and cousins talking in loud, terrible French, how the events of his life had led him to this pew, if he'd had the smallest role in getting himself here. He felt like he'd read it, like he'd been carried to Cravat in his sleep, like his goddamned mother did this for her own entertainment. Not just his mother. All the twats

in his life. It had all been decided by somebody before he was born.

Emile Marcus walked out the side door wearing swim trunks. Rich was relieved to see him and smiled, sitting beneath the tree that smelled like semen. Emile had not expected to see Rich and stopped smiling—he stopped suddenly. The few people here who could hold the kid's hand were a little too weird or too self-absorbed, and it frightened him.

"*Mamma mia,*" Emile said, in the nearest thing he could muster to an exclamation. "I doesn't want to bozzer you." This kid had such a lost, expectant smile it spooked Emile. Rich waved him on, and then got up and sort of pleaded. He was inordinately glad to have another man here among so many women. He pointed out the view. Emile walked over with a wide, stiff gait, and sat down on the pew and tried to think of something to say.

"Everything is okay?"

Rich smiled pathetically and said, "Yeah."

You needed a little bit of swagger if you were going to embark on a real voyage, Emile thought; there was no swagger, no courage showing anywhere in this kid. He tried some local wisdom, spoken slowly, so even an American could understand: "La-mor ay oon mee-stair shee-ont," which meant, "Love is a stinking mystery."

Rich said, "The what?"

Rich already felt kindly toward Emile, he felt protective of the old man, he saw so many signs of weakness and

decay: pewter-colored crowns on the sides of Emile's mouth; condensation inside his wristwatch; his old, drooping balls hanging out of his shorts. He was gray and bent and he'd almost fallen over, earlier, in the driveway, when he'd tried to help Rich with his luggage. With that long scar down his lip and chin, along his throat, Emile looked like someone who, in a rage, had tried to remove his face—something, cut the old one off for the new one underneath it—and had given up halfway through. Rich thought that Emile was someone whose face was profound and could help him fathom aging.

Emile had another thing on his mind. *Was* Gynnie his daughter? The question pricked him constantly, now that he was here. He wasn't even sure he'd gotten it up that night, thirty-three years ago. There were forty-seven women with whom he'd actually achieved his erection. He certainly remembered not getting it up many times, but he vaguely recalled feeling so glorious and happy with Martina—not humiliated.

That summer, Martina came to France for two weeks with her cancerous husband and they stayed in Emile's bed. He and Martina went to art museums, leaving the dying man behind, walked everywhere, cooked, he made portraits of her; on the last night of her visit she tiptoed downstairs and tried to steal the window fan beside him to cure the stifling heat of his bedroom. In the shock of the moment he confessed his true feelings. Maybe she had sex with him for the fan. Maybe she gave in to him because he

loved her, because her husband was croaking, because she needed a good screwing and he let her have it with no expectation of any love in return. He was pretty sure he'd "seeded the soil." He was so furious at her for the vague, obnoxious shrugs, so many times now over the years, when he'd politely demanded to know, in letters, or while visiting her in the States. Even standing on this very spot this morning. "Tell me who I am," he said to her. "I need to know."

"Oh please," she said. "You're ridiculous."

She made him feel like garbage. Sitting beside Rich, Emile realized he had been crying all his life. It was all because of a woman. The woman is the worst creature on the face of the earth, he thought.

"We get drunk tonight," Emile said.

Rich said, "Okay."

"You love her?"

"Yes."

Emile said, "Let me give you one advice: Try to fuck her as much as you can."

GYNNIE SAT SLIGHTLY back from the long table beside her cousin Chantal, who nursed her three-year-old son, Jean-Louis. There was cheese and sausage on one end, blueberries, tea, coffee, and cake on the other. Gynnie asked Chantal, "Does that ever hurt?"

Chantal spoke through her sixteen-year-old cousin, Elena, a deeply tanned girl with wide-set eyes and an awk-

wardly bulging nose, wearing a red bikini. "First time, she cried. He's biting. But then her body feels good."

Chantal's mother-in-law, Marie, across the table, glanced up, her mouth full of food so she appeared to be snarling, and said, "She like it," and went back to eating. Chantal smiled and said, "So." She patted her baby's hair. He lay there, squeezing her other breast like a rubber horn bulb, a little bit of milk on his face, looking at all the women at the table, smiling.

Gynnie leaned over, her hand across his belly and diaper, kissed his face. He stared at her, nipple in his mouth, grinning. "He drinks a lot," Gynnie said. Chantal nodded. Gynnie pointed at his head and said, "I want one of those."

She hadn't touched any food herself, and when Marie looked up again and said, "Bride, eat," and rang Gynnie's plate with the edge of her dirty fork, Gynnie said, "You're all so kind to worry about me," and thought to herself, Fuck you, cow. Everyone thinks I'm an idiot.

Rich came over and sat between Gynnie and Chantal while Chantal continued to nurse; he took some knockwurst and bread. Gynnie wished he'd sat somewhere else. When he reached across her, his armpit smelled. She wished he was staying at the neighbors'. It was clear he belonged here, in the bride's mother's house, less than anyone. She said, "You smell." He said he knew. She watched him shove a knockwurst down.

Gynnie ate yogurt—it was the best yogurt she'd ever eaten in her life. She ate pâté with capers on black bread,

and salami and croissants and jelly and cake, and drank half a pot of espresso, until she could feel the stew coming out her eyeballs, and then she looked for something to crunch in her jaws. She went into the bathroom in their yellow bedroom and threw up everything, and cleaned the toilet and put on the old maroon terry-cloth robe that had been her mother's for twenty years and lay down on the floor beside the bathtub that had been crammed into the alcove next to the linen closet and cried.

Rich had never seen a child with the ability to speak still nursing. The boy stared at Rich, drunkenly. Around the table they were speaking Italian, Dutch, Swiss-German, French, eating chocolate and fruit, drinking black coffee, smoking. Connie and two of his older cousins had been to Annick Goutal in Paris and they smelled of flowers and fruit. The Swiss girls, Lily and Josephine, were braiding each other's hair.

Chantal had an image of infantile fascination on her face, watching the baby watch Rich. What went on at the table between mothers and sons, between a brother and his sisters, between women and babies and men looking on—each was a radiant, impenetrable circle that sealed out the world, made it superfluous. And this Chantal had the most beautiful, full, soft-looking, sweetly moving jugs, like water balloons plumped to the point of ripeness with a golden milky essence.

Rich's sisters smiled at him, trying to get his attention. He winked back.

In a way this place was a kind of heaven. He sat in the seat of all goodness, receiving perfection.

At that exact moment, back across the ocean, Nora Garleck was hearing the pros and cons of a concrete sidewalk storm channel, walking through the very basement Rich had befouled with her the night before.

Never again, he thought, picturing himself getting abused by her, facedown, in the dirt. "Bye-bye, you big horse."

His mother recalled Rich at Jean-Louis's age. "He loved Popeye," she said, out loud, without thinking. "Should we sing 'Popeye the Sailor Man'?" His mother adored him with such intensity. Across from him a woman named Karolyn, with elfin hair, sat smoking. "You like Popeye," she said. Something in the way his mother stared—some piece inside him, some shelf that supported his heart and lungs—then liquefied. Oh, when would he ever grow out of this slavery? Maybe it was the jet lag kicking in, or eating too quickly. The eyes of the women bore through him. He tried shoving a bunch of grapes into his mouth. He got up and moved slowly, making his way through the dark, cold, six-hundred-year-old halls of the house to their bedroom. He went into the bathroom and closed the door and locked it and sat down on the toilet, thinking, Thank God I'm marrying Gynnie and not my mother. Gynnie is perfect for me. Gynnie is cool in every way.

From behind the bathtub where Gynnie lay quietly sobbing she heard Rich enter. She'd been thinking, until his

oafish, dirty sneakers stomped through her moment of healing, that when they got to Morocco there might be an undetectable propane leak in the hotel room and she'd turn blue as a rose, go so silently and painlessly, in her sleep, no more misery ever.

Rich let out the kind of gas that can only be produced by a queasy overnight ocean crossing, squeezed into a coach seat, drinking free suds and wine, igniting that first bellyful of French smorgasbord.

Gynnie sat up and shouted, "What are you doing?"

Rich sat there stunned. He said, "I'm in here! Where did you come from?" He looked at the door he'd locked from inside. On top of his confusion, he could see she'd been sobbing so hard her eyelids looked like walnuts. And when had she ditched her silk kimono for her mom's ratty bathrobe? Her makeup was gone, her eyelids were not the color of the purple robe, but there was a familial resemblance in the two colors.

She said, "Why do you have to do that in here!"

"Where else am I gonna go?" he yelled, and tried to pull his pants up.

"I don't care." She stood in front of him. "Get out of here!" They were the only people in the house and every window was propped wide open; everybody out on the patio heard them screaming. Is this marriage? he thought, running out. Is this typical of what goes on from this point? He held his pants up with one hand, grabbed a magazine in the foyer, and finished his crap down the hall.

. . .

RICH SLEPT THE rest of the afternoon, and sat across from Gynnie at dinner. She'd just come out of the shower and her makeup was off, her face was ashen, her hair hung like fishing line, wrung with flat yellow woodstain, and he took a good look at what he was marrying. A few years earlier she'd had both of her front teeth knocked out in a waterskiing accident; they'd been glued back in but they were "dead," that's how she referred to them. They were the wrong color. Rich wondered then about other dead parts she was transporting, and how he'd find out. Later, after the little kids had gone to bed, he sat there eating cake, the only light from a few candles still burning. He listened to the French street, looked up at the moon, down at the old cement patio stones between his knees. He had a feeling he'd returned to the Old World, to a history that was his, that he'd never lived, a history that overshadowed his life. All day, he'd felt caught in some ancient, familiar rhythm, overwhelmed by women, wondering where his father was.

IN THE MORNING, Rich's mother sat at the kitchen table, speaking to his father on the phone. Martina had brought out a tiny television to watch the report of the storm in the States. After spending the night on the Newark airport floor, Rich's father and brother and best friend took the advice of the Air France representative and drove four hundred miles through the torrent, the downed electrical

wires, falling trees, to Cleveland, Ohio, and when they got there, Cleveland was closed, too. Rich could hear his father's voice, as though it were coming through a garden hose, lashing out that no one insured the plane ticket; his mother sat still, struck silent with embarrassment and rage. The timbre of their fighting sickened him.

She handed Rich the phone, rubbing the skin beneath her right eye over and over, bruised, shaking her head, now happy Rich's father wouldn't be coming.

"Why that cocksucker at the ticket counter didn't tell us sooner is beyond my comprehension," his father said. Anytime Rich's father used the word *cocksucker,* he was probably past caring. He sounded relieved. Rich got a little weepy listening to his father's plan to drive back home and make dinner. Like a lot of people, he'd already let Rich know that staging this thing in Europe was a classic small-minded act of selfishness. His father sang the French national anthem in made-up French words, wished him luck, and hung up. Rich called his machine at home, checked his messages; they told the same story—canceled flights, no apologies. No one else was coming.

When he stepped outside, his aunts were drinking coffee, not talking, looking at each other. Everybody had already heard. Finally his aunt Irene said, "What a shame," in an attempt to mimic real outcry, and then his aunt Patti and cousins Shelley and Tina agreed, Tina sort of scowling slightly, staring at Patti, and then asking, "Does anyone want the last chocolate biscotti? Biscotto?" The sky

was gorgeous—a few huge, flat-bottomed clouds plaqued against the blue-black sky; he could see far out into the valley.

What struck Rich, as his mom picked up half of a croissant and offered it to the baby, was the calm. No one else spoke. The disappointment of being marooned here without half the wedding party? His aunt Irene put her feet up on the table and leaned her head back and closed her eyes, like a girl on vacation who was learning to savor it; she wondered if the airline lost money when weather interfered; nobody knew. Nobody cared that the husbands weren't coming. The "air" being breathed here was the air of relief—not giddy or vindictive relief, but it was awful, all the same. About two hundred years of accumulated married bliss among Rich's mom and four sisters, his cousins, fell away like a scab with no sign of injury beneath it. They were discussing the impact of *Oprah*. It was sickening.

Marriage sucked, he thought. You get married for what, again? You get married because you give up.

His mom went around the driveway on Martina's bicycle, pedaled back and said, "How about for lunch we have a picnic?"

Fuck all of you, Rich thought. I'm not gonna be like this.

There was his mother, making the best of it, getting ready to go back to her miserable marriage. Watching public television when things got hairy, hunchback, face-lift, elastic-waist jeans, yessing Rich's blowhard dad, doing her needlepoint, unable to order her own meal in a restau-

rant, trying to sound brightly engaged in her nonspeaking role in the community theater's *The Music Man,* bragging about their view from the living room back home. There was his father, furious, as usual, but glad to be off the hook, driving back home from the airport to make tomatoes stuffed with rice, so excited he wouldn't have to chance his rectum to foreign foods—he had more interest in his colon than he did in his family; he was more excited for his Winstar cruise than for the wedding, because on the cruise he could flatulate in public, tell his boring stories about the road-crew buddies he'd done community service with after almost going to jail for tax fraud.

Fuck them both, Rich thought.

Emile had been reading the newspaper and tried to lighten the mood and said, "Ha-ha! Rhee-sharrh, we have ze ladies alone. God is a Frenchman. He make you a special wedding!"

Rich went over and looked at a pile of inner tubes Martina rented through an outdoor-adventure company in town. She'd arranged a tubing excursion on the Loire. She had a plug-in twelve-volt air compressor, and every time Rich snapped the valve onto the nipple it popped off. Emile came and stood over him as if he were Rich's father and Rich was his son:

"Pull the metal. You fuck it up."

"Oh, thank you, fuck you. Like you could do it any better."

"Yeah, but you still fuck it up."

Rich felt like punching Emile, but saw, for the first time now, the man smiling.

THEY HAD DINNER in the backyard, by candlelight, beneath a row of linden trees. Some neighbors came to fill the empty seats. They drank local wine from a wooden drum, ate fruit tarts for dessert with strong coffee.

Emile sat beside Gynnie, half-heartedly trying to calm her suspicions about Martina's family's complicity during the war. He knew well enough what she was getting at. "We had our own Holocaust in the Alsace," he wanted to tell her. "We didn't have time to worry about the fucking Poles working in your grandfather's factory in Ulm."

He could see that her mind was over in the trees. She wanted to hear only the terrible stuff.

He wanted to break the cycle of misery he'd passed down. Open your heart, make room for others. He wanted to help her—he didn't know what to do, but she needed to know that everyone loved her, that she had a nasty mother, that no one would stop her from becoming a bitter bride. He lived in a dumb repetition, and she was somehow part of it, a problem that had not been fixed through time.

Out of the corner of Gynnie's eye she saw Rich, at the other end of the table, eating steaming duckbreast off his mother's hot fork, wincing as his mother smiled. She was marrying an idiot. Gynnie simply wanted to find a root cause of her problem, how genocide was linked to her

crabby life maybe, how the stress of a bride was linked to Polish slaughter. She didn't care about her ancestors in Europe. She'd been hoping to uncover some flaw in his evasion, something she could take and pick at and hate him for. She gave up, and when she saw Rich playing with the baby, she felt sad and snuck off to bed.

Later, Rich sat in a chaise at the other end of the table, Jean-Louis asleep across his lap, Chantal sleeping on the other chaise in the dim candlelight.

He and Gynnie weren't speaking, partly because he knew he revolted her right now.

This would be the beginning of a life of real aloneness he hadn't felt since childhood, and he wondered about the baby on his lap, and how the bond that produced this little kid then, in turn, tested women and men. Were the ways we revolt each other infinite? Revulsion did not describe the problem. He felt sorry for himself.

Wherever Nora Garleck was on the earth right now, she did not know how repulsive it was even to kiss her. Maybe no one should ever have to bear the burden of knowing a make-out session could turn so ugly. Maybe intimacy was inherently putrid.

Emile sat down and forced Rich to finish the barrel of wine. Rich shifted the baby and grabbed the wineglass. Emile said he was disappointed, he had thought Rich was going to make a speech tonight. He explained that when a man is ready to commit himself, he needs to let the whole

world know. A man needs to be confident, to stand tall, and if he can't do that, he must pretend, as well as he possibly can, that he knows exactly what he's doing.

He stood up and did a funny imitation of Rich, trying to hold his bride's hand, shaking very badly, his knees buckling.

He placed a wine cork in the candle flame until it was burning, and pulled it out and blew out the flame on the end of the cork, and although it appeared to be smoldering, he grabbed Rich by the back of the head and pressed the cork against Rich's face, wiping it on him. The cork had become charcoal. He explained that a man needed to look distinguished, and in charge, and that with his baby face, maybe what Rich needed was a mustache. In Rich's lap, Jean-Louis slept soundly.

Emile told Rich about his friend Yacob, who had wanted to be a photographer; he was brilliant, but his camera got stolen and in the winter of 1948 he went off to Morocco looking for some wild experiences, and ended up going blind—from fungus (Emile demanded Martina's help translating, and spoke to her in a stern voice Rich hadn't heard before; Martina yelled back at him in French)—and then he killed himself. Rich leaned forward and kept his face taut; the cork was still warm. In the candlelight Rich got a long, careful look at the lines, the bent flesh, the gravity of Emile's disappointments, the ailing glow in his eyes as he looked into Rich's face. Emile never forgave Yacob, he said. Rich smelled the burning cork, the wine on

Emile's breath, the scent of mothballs from the old man's sweater

In his grand gesture to befriend the kid, to lighten the mood, Emile wanted to complete his thought, that a young man needed to believe the miracles of the natural world were within his reach, but he couldn't say it, because he was frightened for Rich and felt responsible. He put his hand on top of Rich's head and smoothed his hair.

"What did I ever do to you?" Rich said, when he walked into the bedroom, surprised to find Gynnie still awake. He stared her in the face, defiant. He couldn't take it anymore.

She said she was sorry. She wondered why he had dirt on his face. She asked him why his pants were wet. He explained that it was from sweat, from where Jean-Louis had slept across his lap; he'd been afraid to move for fear of waking the baby.

Gynnie asked, "Do you like kids?"

She imagined him, for a moment, more mature, with a dark black mustache and beard, a father to her children, a hardened understanding of real responsibility, how it would shape him into something rugged, dependable, steady. She lay there and looked at him as though a mysterious black-haired matador had broken into the room to seduce her.

She said, "Are you mad at me?"

He said, "Are you?"

She said, "You're the best thing that ever happened to me in my life." She waited for him to speak. "The only good thing."

"Are you kidding?"

By the time Rich lay down beside Gynnie they both were feeling that this quarreling was humiliating, and they put their faces together and talked about how they'd been avoiding this moment, and after five minutes they felt lucky and ashamed and were able to kiss. Was this the time and place for him to confess? Confess what, though? He needed to do everybody a favor and stuff that one. The amount of work and excitement and well-wishing had overwhelmed them. The building up of so much in their heads. A lot of the tension was dispelled with that first long kiss. By the time they were making love, they'd quit talking. The entire house knew what was happening. You could hear something that was not creaking but was an indescribable click that was the slats of the bed, the wood being bowed in rhythm. The floor also repeated a faint noise. If you stood on the patio you could hear low speaking of a certain raving nature. You could hear a little of the loony madness of it.

After Rich had walked off the patio, Emile explained to Martina that the morning light, coming from the east, would leave the yard in shadows. He wanted the statues and linden trees on the far end of the yard to be in the background for shooting, and so he showed her how the altar could be turned so that the couple would stand in the sun. He stared at Martina and wondered if his love life was over.

In the quiet of Rich and Gynnie's bedroom, one could

hear the whole house listening. One could hear a sneaker flung at the bedroom door when the door had blown open. Everybody knew that pretty soon they'd be fighting again, and whatever came after that would be hard enough; Aunt Patti, who'd been though a divorce, thought this looked like her first one. So the bride and groom were screwing. Rich and Gynnie went on with the house's good wishes. When they got tired Rich fell over and they did it sideways. After a while, they rested, and then resumed. It was a fine time, when the gist of the fuck had already happened and they were on to higher stuff. Bliss had been achieved. They were riding horse and sulky, through Bliss's pasture. The coming still on hold, prolonged to make them both nuts. There was some moaning. It was a lonely gasping, a gratified finish, soothing, placating. Their own moaning was exciting to both of them and to their aunts and mothers and relatives who were still up drinking wine— who should've been asleep—wondering about love. They sat there after, warm bodies against the old cold wall. At the end they'd done it so hard—Rich fucked Gynnie so hard he forgot he was marrying her.

ACKNOWLEDGMENTS

I NEED TO acknowledge the great debt of gratitude I owe to Daniel Menaker, who made this book happen. Thanks also to: St. Albans School in Washington, D.C.; the Schlesinger Writer-in-Residence at St. Paul's School in Concord, New Hampshire; American University; the Fine Arts Work Center; and the Hill School in Pottstown, Pennsylvania.

PENGUIN BOOKS

SAM THE CAT

Matthew Klam lives in Washington, D.C. In 1999 he was named one of the twenty best young fiction writers in America by the *New Yorker*. He is an O'Henry Award winner and a contributor to *The New York Times Magazine*. You can contact him at: www.matthewklam.com